Alice slept and dreamed about Camilla. Camilla was laughing and whispering, *"You'd better lock the door. It's wisest."* What a queer laugh Camilla had developed: throaty and malicious. She was actually turning the key in the lock and laughing in that deep gurgle.

It was so peculiar that it wakened Alice. She opened her eyes wide, trying to throw off the nightmare. The square of her window was scarcely less dark than the rest of the room, but something was moving in the darkness. It was the curtains swaying in and out, the rings on which they hung clinking faintly.

Then there was a movement near the door and a voice whispered, *"Camilla's here. Isn't that a joke?"* There was that awful throaty laugh again. It hadn't been in her dream after all; it existed in reality. . . .

THE
BROODING
LAKE

(Orig. Title: Lamb to the Slaughter)

by
DOROTHY EDEN

ace books
A Division of Charter Communications Inc.
A GROSSET & DUNLAP COMPANY
360 Park Avenue South
New York, New York 10010

THE BROODING LAKE

Copyright © 1953, by Macdonald & Co. Ltd.

An ACE BOOK
by special arrangement with the author.

To A. T. D.
for always reminding me
of the importance of laughter

I

THE RAIN HAD increased to a steady downpour when Alice climbed out of the bus. The bus driver, his collar pulled up over his ears, ran around to the luggage compartment to get her bags.

"West coast weather," he said in a friendly voice designed for the hearing of the rest of the passengers. "You'll get used to it. Staying long?"

"Felix, you fool!" Alice hissed under her breath. "What are you doing here?" Aloud she said aloofly, "I haven't decided yet."

The bus was full of passengers on their way to the glacier hotel. After a journey of several hours around tortuous mountain roads they would not be amused at their driver dallying with one of his female passengers at a cottage gate.

He leaned over to push open the rickety gate. Water dripped off the long lock of black hair that hung over his forehead. He looked as if he had grown as impervious to it as a duck.

"Give my love to Camilla," he said.

Then he leaped into the bus, started the engine with a roar, and moved off down the wet winding road.

Alice was left alone in the green gloom. Refusing to think of Felix and his unexpected disturbing presence, she turned to the cottage. With the thick rain and the masses of bush cut back from the road, but threatening, by the luxuriance of its growth, to return to its domains at any time, one had a curious underwater feeling. Beyond the treetops the mountains, lost in haze, towered. One was at the bottom of a lake and the world grew up above one. It was exciting and unreal and very, very wet.

And why hadn't Camilla, who must have seen the bus stop, come to open the door?

Alice hurried up the slippery path, half overgrown with the reaching eager fern tendrils, and, depositing her bags on the doorstep, thumped loudly on the door.

It was a small wooden cottage, discolored with damp, old and tumbledown. A hundred yards away, beyond the trees, Alice could see the bright new yellow school shining outlandishly in this world of subdued green and gray. She remembered Camilla writing, "We've got a brand-new school, but the house I'm expected to live in—well, you should come and see it. I've prettied it up with cretonne and things, and I light huge fires to keep out the damp, but I still go through the floor here and there, and when it really rains everything that will hold water is put out to catch the drips. They want me to go and live at the hotel, but in spite of everything I like it here. It's cheaper and I have more fun."

2

Standing with the rain running down her neck, it occurred to Alice to wonder what fun Camilla could have living alone in this dreary little place. But Camilla had never been the dull kind. Had she been shipwrecked on a desert island she would have rustled up a man or two to amuse her.

Obviously, from Felix's parting remark, she was running true to form.

But where was she now that she didn't come to open the door? Alice knocked again, and waited. The rain continued to run down her neck. A bird suddenly swooped over her with a harsh squawk. It settled on the gate and gazed at her unwinkingly. It was a kea, she realized, one of the squat gray mountain birds with curved cruel parrot beaks that preyed on sheep and newly born lambs. If she were to move away it would come and peck inquisitively at her luggage. It had a malevolent gaze that seemed peculiarly in keeping with the drenched gloom.

It's putting a spell on me, Alice thought; and suddenly impatient with Camilla's dilatoriness, she rattled at the doorknob. The kea squawked again and, spreading its powerful wings, the underparts of which were iridescent with color, flew away.

The doorknob beneath Alice's fingers refused to turn. The door was locked.

What had happened? Camilla was expecting her, she knew, because she had had that note saying, "Thrilled you're coming. Will be here to meet you. Don't mind the bus." And then the postscript that was so typical of Camilla: "You must meet all my boyfriends. It's a hell of a joke, and am I getting into hot water!"

All one could suppose now was that Camilla had got into hot water, for obviously she had forgotten to keep her promise to be there to meet Alice.

Suddenly angry with her for her thoughtlessness, Alice stepped off the doorstep and leaned over to push up one of the windows. It was too wet to plod around to the back. If the window opened she would get into the house that way.

It did. With a rickety rattle the frame slid up, and at the same moment a high sharp voice from within cried, "Go away! Go away quick!"

Alice almost fell back among the dripping fern. She clutched the windowsill, her heart pounding. It was stupid of her to be frightened; this was Camilla's house, silly empty-headed harmless lively Camilla. There was nothing queer or ominous in that room into which she couldn't see for the gloom. Someone was playing a trick on her.

"Camilla!" she called rather shakily. "Is that you? Are you having a joke?"

There was a movement in the gloom. Or was it her imagination that something more dark than the darkness of the corner moved?

Then abruptly, in that nerve shattering way, the small high voice screamed, "Go away!" And all at once a cat leapt on the sill, mewing, and the room beyond it was alive with the sudden sharp flapping of wings.

Alice did, for a moment, subside weakly into the wet ferns. She was laughing breathlessly. That thing—it was a parrot of some kind. Camilla must keep it for company, perhaps purposely to startle guests. She had always loved practical jokes. In a moment she would appear, splitting her sides with laughter.

"Camilla, you wretch!" Alice muttered.

The cat leaned down from the sill, mewing piteously. Alice scrambled up to stroke it. It sounded as if it was hungry. It was a big ginger-colored Persian with a plumed tail like the waving toi-toi grass in the bush. It was a magnificent creature, but how had Camilla come to neglect to feed it?

Alice was conscious of her first stirring of alarm. It really did look as if Camilla was not there, after all, and this was no practical joke. She stuck her head through the open window, and then resolutely climbed over the sill. The room in which she found herself was dark with the overhanging bush and the gloomy day now drawing to a close. Alice fumbled her way to the door and felt for a light switch. There was none. She went out into the little hall, but still her searching fingers could find none. Then her gaze went to the lamp hanging from the ceiling. Good gracious, it was old-fashioned. Camilla had said the house was antique, but she had never mentioned the lack of electricity.

As she felt in her bag for matches something smooth and quick sidled against her legs. She gave a gasp, seeing a small black shadow retreating quickly. Again there was the sharp clapping of wings and the little eerie voice said, "Go away quick! Quick!"

"I'll do nothing of the kind," Alice retorted, and struck a match to light the lamp.

The soft illumination showed the room: the big brick fireplace with the dead remnants of a fire, the low chairs and the large low settee covered with bright cushions, the pictures on the walls strategically placed to hide the discolored spots in the wallpaper, the large white rug in front of the fireplace, the gilt-framed mirror that gave back a dusky lamplit reflection of the room. The illusion of luxury was a triumph on the part of Camilla. It made her seem very near. Alice, looking around curiously, gave a confident, "Yoo hoo! Cam! I'm here!"

The cat rubbed around her legs, mewing. The black active shadow leaped onto the arm of a chair, and at last Alice saw what it was: a magpie with bright eyes and a long wicked beak. She gave a low astonished chuckle. *Shades of Edgar Allan Poe. Fancy old Camilla keeping a magpie. She must have been lonely in her mountain fastness.*

But where the devil was she now? Alice left the room to wander through the dusk-filled house. The rain drummed on the roof as she opened the doors of bedrooms, two side by side, one obviously Camilla's because an open drawer showed underclothing dripping out (again as clear evidence of Camilla as her fingerprints). The other one had the bed made up neatly, and there was a vase of some bright red bush flowers on the dressing-table. This would be her room, and it showed that Camilla was expecting her. She went on down the narrow hallway to what must be the kitchen. The door to this room was shut. She felt for the knob in the gloom. At the same moment that she turned it there came the sound of a door at the back softly clicking shut.

Camilla at last! Alice flung open the door eagerly.

"I say, I've got here before you!"

No one answered. The room, with its old-fashioned coal range and high mantelpiece, its cheer-fully ticking clock and rain beating on the small window, was empty.

Who had come in? Or gone out?

Alice ran to the back door and opened it. A path led into the green dripping bush. There were hollows that could have been footprints rapidly filling with water, and wet mud on the doorstep. But none of it made sense, because there was no sign of anyone anywhere.

Alice sat down rather shakily on one of the kitchen chairs. She realized now that someone must have been in the house all the time while she had been knocking at the front door. Whoever it was had stayed until the last possible minute, probably hoping that she would give up and go away. When she had not done that the intruder had been forced to make a hasty exit.

But who had it been? And where was Camilla?

The cat suddenly rubbed around her legs again, repeating its petition for food. Alice forced herself to get up and open a cupboard. All the time she had the feeling that she was being watched.

She found some remnants of cold lamb and a jug of milk that was distinctly sour. Sour? How could that be? Camilla surely would get fresh milk every day.

The cat, anyway, should have some of the cold lamb to keep it quiet. She herself, if it came to that, was pretty hungry. She had traveled all day on cups of tea.

But Camilla would arrive presently and they would have a meal. Probably she had gone out to get provisions. The cupboards were almost empty. There was half a loaf of stale bread in a tin and the end of a pound of butter. The bread looked at least three days old. That, and the sour milk—almost as if Camilla hadn't eaten for three days. And the hungry cat—almost as if she hadn't been in the cottage.

In the gloomy little kitchen Alice felt the prickles of apprehension going over her again. Who had gone out at the back door in a hurry and disappeared into the bush?

Was there someone watching her through the window now? She couldn't rid herself of that conviction. Almost in a panic she hurried back to the living-room, warm with lamplight, and pulled down the blinds. Then, with her courage partially restored, she resolved to search the house thoroughly. Because Camilla wasn't far away. She was sure of that. In the bathroom there was a faint odor of carnation, and Camilla's towel and face cloth hanging on a rail. In the bedroom her clothes hung in the wardrobe. There was evidence of her everywhere, yet she was not there.

But someone had closed the back door.

In the kitchen Alice picked up a desk calendar. There was a leaf for each day, but today's date had not been turned up. It remained at yesterday's. And the number, the sixteenth of January, had a ring around it in red and an exclamation mark. What had been happening to Camilla yesterday?

Alice remembered Camilla's habit of scrawling notes everywhere to jog a lazy memory. She turned back the leaves, and sure enough on the previous day there was a note, *Don't forget cat's meat;* and on the fourteenth, *D tonight*. The twelfth and thirteenth were blank, but on the eleventh there was a hasty note, written, obviously, under excitement or stress, *D is so impetuous*.

That was all.

Who was D? Whoever he was, Alice was left with no doubt that he was the cause of Camilla's absence.

There was a clicking on the floor as the magpie hopped into the kitchen. It stood still and regarded Alice with its head on one side, its long sharp beak pointing sideways. Then it said in an intimate friendly voice, "Hello, darling. How long can you stay?"

The absurdity of it (the words breathed Camilla) broke Alice's tension, and she began to laugh. At the same moment there was a rap on the window pane, and she was momentarily conscious of a pale shape of a face with hair plastered down with rain looking in. Before she had time for alarm the back door opened and Felix walked in.

"What are you doing in the dark, darling?" he said pleasantly. "Where's Camilla?"

The relief from her tension was so great that Alice almost had a desire to weep on his shoulder. After what had happened in Christchurch it was the last shoulder she would have chosen, but it was so wonderful to see another human being in this oddly deserted house.

"No one," she said, "has less idea where Camilla is than I have."

He threw off his wet oilskins and pushed back the dripping lock of hair off his forehead. His skin shone with rain and his eyes shone with his peculiar mocking merriment that tonight was particularly irritating.

"Is that so? Did she know you were coming?"

Alice looked at him accusingly.

"And you knew, too."

"Naturally. Camilla is my friend. Your friends are mine, darling."

"Don't call me darling. I thought we'd settled all that sort of thing."

"So we had."

The lock of hair falling over his bony brow was achingly familiar.

"Then what on *earth* are you doing here playing at being a bus driver?" Alice asked angrily.

"It's a part that appeals to me. And one has to eat, you know."

"But why *here*? And why a *bus* driver?"

"Dar—Alice, you must get out of the habit of speaking in italics. People will guess you're an actress. I mean, were an actress. And is there anything wrong with my pursuing my trade in this part of the world? The west coast of New Zealand is a truly magnificent spot. The scenery couldn't be excelled: the snowpeaks, the valleys and lakes, that incredible glacier coming down into the heart of the bush like one of the mountains letting down its hair. As for the women—"

"Spare me the travel talk," Alice interrupted. "Was it your suggestion that Camilla write asking me to come over?"

"As for the women," Felix went on imperturbably, "they are wonderful. Your friend Camilla alone is a witch. Do you know, she has the whole male population at her feet, including the odd tourists who wander this way. How does she do it?"

"She's always done that," said Alice impatiently. "One day she'll get herself into trouble. And not the kind you think I mean. You haven't answered my question."

"You mean, breach of promise, or an attack by a jealous lover, or—"

"Felix!"

He looked at her, his black eyes deliberately penitent.

"All right, darling, it was on my suggestion that Camilla have you over. Here I am eating three good meals a day and I thought you might be starving. Little Alice mustn't starve, I said."

"So it was pity," said Alice.

"Purely pity," he agreed. "Camilla understood. She's a—"

"All right, then, you were right. At the present moment I am starving. Where is Camilla likely to be?"

"I don't know. Maybe up at the Thorpe farm. Or across at the store. Or having drinks at the hotel. But you said she was expecting you today. Unless she has made a mistake in the day. She hadn't much of a memory, had she? She was always scribbling notes or tying something around her finger."

"That's true," said Alice. "Then I suppose I can expect her home soon. Are you going to wait?"

"One would hardly call that a cordial invitation," Felix murmured. "One would give a warmer invitation to a cat." He stooped and swung the yellow cat against his chin, and the creature settled down in his arms with a deep purr of content. "But no one could be less thin-skinned than I. I stay if I wish, invitation or not. We'll get a meal, shall we? By that time, Camilla will be home.''

"But—''

He waved his hand and the cat leapt to the floor.

"No polite protest. It's not the first time I've done this. Lazy little devil, Miss Camilla Mason. If you're staying long you'll find you have to do the housework. Are you staying long?''

Alice felt too tired and too glad of his company in this uneasy rain-washed gloom to hold out against him any longer. After all, they had always been friends. It had only been when they had imagined that they were in love that they had begun to fight.

"I haven't decided. And it can be of no possible interest to you.''

"Why don't you go back to England?''

"No,'' she said sharply. "You know I won't do that.''

"But your parents—''

"Felix, for heaven's sake, if there's one thing that doesn't become you it's being a hypocrite. You know as well as I do that my father would have to sandwich me somewhere between the wing structure and the undercarriage of his new plane, and I'd simply be an embarrassment to my mother. I don't even know where she is. It was Cannes the last time I heard, but it could easily be New York or Kingston, Jamaica, by now. It's not their fault. They weaned themselves of having a daughter when they sent me out here during the war. It's a thing that's happened, that's all. I don't want to talk about it.''

"But at least—''

"Felix, if you mention money to me again I'll slap

your face. I'm me. I'm an individual. I look after myself. I *like* things the way they are. I like being in New Zealand. I've been homesick for it ever since I went back to England for the first time. And I don't need pity from a broke producer.''

''At the moment,'' said Felix mildly, ''I wasn't giving you pity.''

His mouth was curving in that old tender smile that didn't mean a thing, that was merely an ornament on his lean, clever, sardonic face.

''Then what are you giving me?''

''Admiration for your stubbornness. At home you could have everything. Here what have you?''

''Rain down my neck,'' said Alice with sudden grim humor. ''And if you got Camilla to ask me over here just to tell me all over again to go home you've been wasting your time.''

He grinned suddenly. ''Then go and change or you won't live either to go home or to bus-ride with me. I'll have to write your obituary notice. 'A lamb to the slaughter' I'll call it. That's what you look like. A little soft white lamb. Haven't you heard the keas screeching? They prey on silly little lambs. Well, go and change while I put the bacon on. And don't,'' he added, ''put on anything too glamorous. I can't stand it if you start looking glamorous.''

Obedience to his direction after months on the stage had become a habit. As Alice went into the little bedroom to change, her thoughts went back to Camilla. How had she and Felix progressed? They would be a good pair in that their emotions were apt to get out of control and they enjoyed the semblance of being in love. Even at school Camilla had thrived on emotional complications. To her they were the spice of life. With great ingenuity and innocent she scrambled out of one affair and plunged into another. Alice had always kept her emotions under control. Until she had met Felix. But that lapse had been temporary. She had herself in hand again now. She would neither be emotionally untidy like Camilla nor flirtatious like her mother, nor careless and gay and false like Felix. But why had Felix interfered and got her over here? Why hadn't he been able to let well alone? Did he have a conscience about her? That was not necessary. She was twenty-four and mature enough to handle this sort of thing.

"I say, Alice!" His voice came from the kitchen, breaking into her thoughts. "This is extraordinary."

With a little sharp chill Alice's sense of comfort left her and suddenly she was back to her feeling of apprehension, to the odd premonition that the kea screeching on the gate and the magpie saying "Go away, quick" had given her.

"What's extraordinary?"

"There's practically no food and everything's stale. Did you say Camilla knew you were arriving today?"

"Yes; she answered my letter."

"I would say this milk is at least two days old. Phoo! Why didn't she get fresh milk?"

The red ring around the calendar was for yesterday. Was that the last day on which Camilla had got fresh milk?

Alice hastily zipped her housecoat and went out to the kitchen.

"Someone shut the door when I was in the front room before," she said breathlessly. "At least, I could have sworn it was the door shutting. As if someone had been snooping."

He surveyed her with his brooding eyes. He said nothing.

"Do you think I imagined it?"

"Alas, no. It could so easily be. Camilla had admirers."

Alice said irrelevantly, "No bus driver would say *alas*."

He raised his brows.

"You have an analytical mind. I've always said that that's your curse. It doesn't go with your little white-lamb look. But if you must be analytical let's be analytical about Camilla, who hasn't left us any fresh milk or bread."

"If someone was looking for her why should they run away?"

"Camilla adores intrigues. If you knew her at school you must know that."

"Yes, I do," Alice admitted. Camilla was not beautiful. She was not even pretty. She had carroty-blonde hair and light-green eyes, freckles on her short nose, and her mouth was large and full-lipped. But she had a way of paying deep absorbed attention to everything one said. It was very deceptive, that air of attention, for often Camilla's mind could not be farther from what was being said. But a man wouldn't find that out at once. By the time he did Camilla would have been giving him her initial chaste kisses. She was a scamp, but one quite without malice. One always ended by reluctantly forgiving her for her outrageous behavior and remaining her friend.

But she was illogically sorry if Felix had fallen under her spell. For all his sardonic outlook he could be vulnerable. She knew that.

He had got the stove going and had bacon frying in a pan. There was a cloth on the table and knives and forks. He looked so much at home that he might have lived there. Ungrateful Camilla to be out with another man.

"Elderly bacon and burnt toast is the menu," he said.

He had made the toast over the fire, impatiently, without waiting for the flame to die down. It was blackened, but to Alice's hungry nostrils it smelled delicious.

"Do you stay up at the hotel?" she asked.

"Every second night. I bring the bus down one day and back to Hokitika the next."

"Do you like bus driving?"

"As well as you like shopkeeping."

"How did you know I was in a shop?"

"I made it my business to find out what happened to all the cast. Gloria Matson married a Hawkes Bay sheep-farmer, Madeleine Grey went to Australia, Guy Faulkner worked his passage home, Neville Britton started in insurance, Felix Dodsworth is driving a bus, and Alice Agatha Ashton—were you named after maiden aunts, darling?—sells gloves and stockings over a counter, and gives the wrong change."

"I do not! At least—"

"She never had to have a head for money. She has wealthy parents. I am now quoting Camilla. Camilla says, 'Why didn't you marry Alice, you goop? But honestly I'm glad you didn't.' Close quote."

Alice colored fiercely.

"Do you always eat with Camilla on your night at the hotel?" she countered.

"Certainly not. It wouldn't be convenient to Camilla." He put another piece of bacon on her plate. "Tonight I came to see you."

"Why? Really, Felix, we had this all out in Christchurch, and it's not the slightest use—"

But her heated statement was interrupted by a sharp knocking at the front door.

Camilla at last! With relief Alice exclaimed gaily, *"Whence is that knocking?"* Felix, following her into the hall, added sonorously, *"How is't with me when every noise appalls me?"*

Alice giggled and whispered, "Fine bus driver you are!"

But before she had reached the end of the short hall her relief had left her. Of course the person at the door would not be Camilla, for why should Camilla knock at her own door?

II

THE MAN WHO stood dripping in the rain was short and squarish. He peered forward, trying to see them in the dark.

"Is Camilla not in?" he asked in a soft pleasant voice.

Alice liked his voice. She liked everything about him because she welcomed his intrusion at that particular moment. It would have been more than she could have borne to have gone over that long weary argument with Felix again. When someone had ceased to love you, to argue about it was tasting ashes.

Felix moved forward.

"Oh, is that you, Dundas?" Felix's friendliness embraced everyone. As a bus driver he must be a staggering success. "Camilla doesn't seem to be home."

"Where is she? Do you know?"

The soft voice had sharpened a little. (*He's one of Camilla's boyfriends and he's jealous,* Alice thought.)

"Your guess is as good as mine," Felix said amiably. "Come in. Meet Miss Alice Ashton, Camilla's guest. This is Dundas Hill, Alice."

Alice gravely shook hands. She was aware of a round, fresh-colored, surprisingly young face beneath gray hair. The man's eyes were light-colored and smiling. He looked very pleasant. Dundas. *D is so impetuous*, she thought. But Dundas Hill with his solid figure and firm handshake looked far from impetuous.

"Camilla's guest, you said?" he repeated. "But doesn't Camilla know she's here?"

"Now you ought to know better than me what Camilla's memory is," Felix answered. His eyes had their merry sardonic look again. "Are you coming in out of the rain?"

"*Quoth the raven, nevermore!*" came the hoarse startling voice of the magpie.

Dundas gave a start.

"Great Scott, that bird!"

Felix was laughing.

"Haven't you heard him on that one? I don't know whether Camilla was searching for atmosphere or just suffering from a hangover when she taught him that."

"He's uncanny," Alice said.

"Webster," Felix introduced him, as the bird skittered over the polished floor.

"After the dictionary?" Alice asked in appreciation.

Dundas had taken off his wet coat and followed them into the kitchen. He still looked upset and anxious, as if he took Camilla's absence more seriously than did Felix. Perhaps it hurt him more that Camilla apparently had other affairs in her life. He looked as if he would be the sensitive kind. In spite of his gray hair he didn't look more than forty. Of course, he would be in love with Camilla. That was a foregone conclusion.

"But didn't Camilla know you were coming today, Miss Ashton?" he persisted.

"Indeed she did. I had a letter from her saying she would be here."

"A letter, eh?" Dundas' voice sounded heavy and serious. His eyes looked puzzled.

The rain seemed to have become heavier and was pouring in a steady stream on the roof. A wet patch was growing larger in the ceiling. It was quite dark outside. The reflection of their faces hung in the gloom. Alice could see her own ruffled head, Felix's high black one, his tilted eyes narrowed with laughter, and Dundas' bright cheeks and worried eyes. If Camilla were to be coming home by the bush track now she would look in at them, and Alice could imagine her lighthearted chuckle at the complicated emotions she caused. Something would happen to her one day. One couldn't go on playing like that always.

Perhaps, came the chilling thought, something had already happened.

Dundas was pursuing the subject with great seriousness.

"If Camilla said she would be here, why isn't she? Did she leave things ready for you?"

"The bed's made in the spare room, that's all." She went on nervously, "But she must be here. Her clothes are everywhere. She might have gone away for a night, that would be all."

"That must be it," Dundas agreed. "She's at some farm and can't get back. The rivers are flooded, you know. That would mean she wouldn't be here until the morning, and not even then unless the rain stops."

As he spoke a drip suddenly fell from the damp spot in the ceiling onto his neck. He rubbed his neck vigorously.

"This house is a disgrace. We shouldn't be letting anyone live in it."

"Dundas is the school chairman," Felix explained to Alice. "He takes his duties seriously. Quite rightly, too. This house *is* a disgrace." He lit a cigarette and went on, "So we've decided Camilla is marooned, have we? Probably you're right, too. She could have gone away for a couple of days. That would explain the stale milk. Then in that case I'll get along. Perhaps you'd be wiser to come up to the hotel tonight, Alice."

Alice shook her head.

"Oh, no, I'll stay here. I'm crazy about the place already. It's mysterious."

"It's very unhealthy," said Dundas. "I don't think you should stay here. Will you come over to my place? I have my daughter there."

Felix's merry eyes twinkled at her. Alice shook her head.

"No. Thank you very much, but I'd rather stay here. If Camilla doesn't turn up by tomorrow I'll decide then what I'll do."

"She must turn up by tomorrow," said Felix, "otherwise we'll think she's in trouble."

"Nonsense! What trouble would she be in?" Dundas said.

"I can think of several kinds. Alas!" He shrugged himself into his wet mackintosh. "Good night, Alice. Sleep well."

"Oh, I shall. Don't worry about me."

She followed him to the door. He stood a moment in the dark cool air, full of wet bush scents.

"Sure?" he said.

"Of course. What do you have here that could frighten me? Tigers?"

He leaned to kiss her lightly on the cheek.

"Nice girl," he said.

Then he plunged off into the darkness, and Alice turned to see Dundas watching her. What interesting eyes he had, round and soft and kind and peculiarly innocent.

"He's very forward," she said mildly, rubbing her cheek. "But what's a kiss for me? After all, he's in love with Camilla."

Alice always treated any subject airily, but momentarily she was sorry about this one, for Dundas looked shocked.

All at once he said emphatically, "You can't stay here alone. You'll have to come over to my place."

"But why?" She looked at him seriously. "Good heavens, I really believe you think something has happened to Camilla."

"Nothing of the kind. Camilla's the kind to look after herself. It's this dreadful house. Look at the water coming through the ceiling. It's not habitable in a heavy rain. It's a shocking place to expect a visitor to stay."

Alice had always disliked being organized. Quite

apart from her irritation over that she had no intention whatever of leaving the cottage. Camilla might be home any minute. Even if she were not Alice had a curious feeling that she had to stay.

Dundas Hill, for all his kindness, was just a trifle pompous from being the local school chairman.

"No, thank you," she said lightly but definitely. "It's very kind of you, but I prefer to stay here."

He stared at her with his worried intensity.

"Are you determined about that?"

"Quite."

"Then I might as well go." He opened the door to the dark night. He seemed reluctant to leave her. She was almost reluctant to let him go. His square solid figure was reassuring and gave her a feeling of safety.

"I hope you will come over and see my studio some time. Margaretta will make you a cup of tea." His voice had a velvety quality. It made Alice think of deep soft plush. It was extremely soothing to one's nerves.

"I'd like to very much," Alice answered sincerely.

"That's if you stay, of course."

"But I intend to stay," Alice heard herself saying definitely. She had made that decision all at once. There was something intriguing and unassociated with herself going on here. It was a relief to be an observer instead of a participator in a drama. Quite apart from the assistance it might be to Camilla, it would do her good to stay.

"I only meant if—if you can put up with the discomfort of our atrocious weather."

Curiously enough Alice had the impression that he had meant to say something entirely different.

"And you're very small to stay here alone," he added unexpectedly.

"Small?"

"Exquisitely small. Like my ladies."

"Your ladies?" The nice little man was inexplicable.

"I have a collection of Dresden china figures. My ladies, I call them. You shall see them when you come over."

Alice watched him disappear into the dark, and suddenly all her apprehension was back. It had been easy enough, with the two men here, to talk lightly about the probable reasons for Camilla's absence, but alone in the little half-lighted cottage she had an odd uncomfortable feeling that something was very much wrong. If the rain and the swollen rivers prevented Camilla from getting back couldn't she have telephoned the hotel and had a message sent up? Of course, she might not have been able even to get to a telephone, Alice told herself reasonably. It *must* be all right.

The cat rubbed around her legs. It was still hungry, poor thing, after its meager meal. She picked it up, hugging it for comfort. It began to purr, fixing its adoring pale golden eyes on her. Camilla's eyes had that same sleepy adoring expression whenever she had wished. The thought of that suddenly made Alice shiver; she didn't know why. The sensation had come over her overwhelmingly that she would never see the warm sleepy light in Camilla's eyes again.

When she went to bed, however, the thought of

25

Camilla went out of her mind and it was Felix's face that haunted her. Felix, long and thin in Malvolio's ridiculous garb; Felix a wistful Hamlet torturing one with his beautiful yearning voice; Felix in the proud crimson and gold of Caesar; Felix an astonishingly convincing Falstaff, with the cushions under his doublet inclined to slip; Felix shouting at them all, "You're bad, bad, bad! I loathe and detest you!" Or saying caressingly, "Just conceivably this may be good. But don't let the thought go to your heads."

They had all slaved for him. They had all said he was wasting his talents dragging a small company around the world. They had stuck to him until the last gasp, until there wasn't even enough money to pay their passages back to England. In a little theater in Christchurch, New Zealand, the curtain came down for the last time, and the members of the company gaily and courageously decided to go their several ways.

That night was three months away now. Alice thought she had contrived to forget it sufficiently to take an interest in her new life. She thought that scene of Felix and herself sitting over a table in a small café had lost its power to make her weep. But here it was again, the red-checked tablecloth, not very clean, the grilled steak and bacon Felix had insisted on her having because he wanted to leave her with the memory of her having one square meal.

She couldn't eat the food. She cut the bacon into small pieces and left it on her plate growing cold.

"We're through, aren't we, Felix?" she said miserably. "Not just the company. You and me."

"It looks like it," he said.

"But, Felix—" She looked at his face and saw the closed stubborn look that she knew would not change. It had been there when he had told her that the company was splitting up and she must go back to England. She, of them all, had no need to starve deliberately. Actually, none of them needed to starve, but again only she had no need to seek some uncongenial occupation.

If only she had known how much of that scene was due to the fact that Felix would not impose poverty on her and how much it was because he no longer loved her. It was something of each, she knew. He was too sensitive about his lack of money and prospects, but also he liked and admired women. She would not be the first nor the last with whom he was in love. Sadly, she knew the whole lovely thing between them was a failure, and it was no use arguing. In any case Felix, in this mood, would not be argued with. She had heard his caressing voice saying "Little Alice" for the last time.

"If we could get drunk," she said wistfully, "we could face this with a flourish."

He grinned suddenly, his long face lighting up.

"Then let's get drunk, but it will have to be on beer. I've got exactly nine shillings and twopence."

But the beer had made Alice more sad and she had begun singing in her clear mournful voice,

"He is dead and gone, lady;
He is dead and gone.
At his head a grass-green turf,
At his heels a stone."

People had turned to look at them, and Felix had patted her hand gently and said, "Come on home."

In a way those had been his last words to her. "Come on home." *They should have been beautiful words,* she thought drearily.

But home to her, at that moment, had been a shabby hotel room. Felix had left her at the door. She hadn't seen or heard of him again until today. She had been priding herself that she could recover as easily as he from a love affair, but when she had seen him in the bus the unexpectedness of it had left her speechless and trembling. She had wanted to giggle at the absurdity of it; she might have known Felix would be versatile and original in his methods of earning a living. But instead she had frozen into herself, and it was only at the end of the long journey that she had been able to develop an airy casual attitude towards him.

Lying in the narrow bed listening to the rain on the roof, Alice decided that that was the attitude she would maintain so long as she remained here with Camilla. For Felix's interest in her was now only brotherly or paternal or something cold-blooded like that.

He had been interested enough to want to see her again, but it had been only out of pity. Pity! What a horrible word. He and Camilla had planned this between them. It was Camilla now who occupied his mind. But where was Camilla, the flighty little witch?

On that last puzzled thought Alice fell asleep.

She didn't know how much later it was that the yellow cat startled her badly by jumping on the bed.

"Hello, puss," she murmured. "What do you know about Camilla?"

The rain had stopped and the silence after the steady downpour seemed unreal. Alice leaned over to open the little window, eager to smell the fresh mountain air. It was still completely dark. The window pane brushed against a branch of fern, and cool drops of moisture fell on her hand. At the same time there was a rustle and crackle in the bush. Alice drew back, startled.

"Who's there?" she called.

There was no answer and no other sound. Yet now, fully awake, she was conscious of a queer dream that she had been having that someone was moving about in the house. The cat's arrival had woken her from it. Or had it been a dream? Perhaps it had been Camilla arriving home, creeping in quietly so as not to disturb her.

Fully awake, Alice knew she wouldn't sleep again until she had investigated. Resignedly she lit a candle and got up.

Camilla's bed was empty. The fragment of peach-colored silk still hung out of her drawer. If Camilla were not a natually untidy person it would look as if she had gone away in a hurry, throwing things into a bag. Where *had* she gone?

All at once Alice remembered the calendar with the scribbled notes on it, and a thought occurred to her. If Camilla made notes to jog her memory perhaps there would be notes for the future, too.

She went out to the kitchen and groped on the mantelpiece where she had put the calendar. She couldn't feel it, and finally stood on a chair to look at the accumulated debris, matchboxes, cigarettes, old letters and dust on the high mantelpiece. It was then that she saw the envelope addressed in large printing to herself.

How silly! Here was the answer to the problem all the time and she hadn't known. Camilla might have put it in a more conspicuous spot, of course. Probably she had, and it had slipped down, or the magpie, in his short flights, had knocked it over.

She tore open the envelope and extracted the note. It, too, was written in large printing, the kind Camilla probably taught her pupils in school.

DEAR ALICE,

I AM BEING MARRIED. ISN'T IT A SCREAM! IT'S ALL VERY SECRET AND HUSH HUSH BECAUSE WE DON'T WANT A FUSS. SORRY NOT TO BE THERE WHEN YOU ARRIVED, BUT THIS IS THE WAY THINGS HAVE SUDDENLY HAPPENED. HE WON'T LISTEN TO ANYTHING BUT RUSHING ME TO THE ALTAR. THE WISE MAN DOESN'T TRUST ME! I JUST HADN'T TIME TO DO A THING. WE'RE CATCHING A PLANE TOMORROW. HE HAS BOOKINGS HE CAN'T MISS. I'M IN A DITHER. I CAN'T MAKE SENSE. BUT YOU'LL HEAR FROM ME AGAIN. I'LL SEND FOR THE REST OF MY CLOTHES LATER. I AM GLORIOUSLY HAPPY.

LOVE,
CAMILLA

III

WITH THE PROBLEM of Camilla's disappearance at last solved, Alice slept. She was awakened in the morning by the now familiar sound, a hammering on the door. She scrambled into a housecoat and slippers, hastily smoothed her hair, and went to open the door.

Felix stood there. He had on his uniform, and beyond him at the gate stood the bus, his odd new stage property, with its engine running.

"Just on my way," he said. "Can't stop. Any news of Camilla?"

"Yes. She's gone off to get married."

"No!" His lean face was quite still. "How do you know?"

"There was a letter for me on the mantelpiece. I didn't find it until late. Wait, I'll show it to you."

She watched as he read the letter. At the end his brows drew together. He handed it back.

"I don't believe it," he said flatly. "Anyone could print that. Couldn't they?"

Before she could produce her confused thoughts he had turned to go down the path, calling over his shoulder, "Don't go away. I'll see you tomorrow night and we'll talk."

She noticed passengers peering out of the bus at the young woman in a housecoat with whom the driver was so audibly making a date. If only they knew the date was merely to talk about another woman! Though even that was better, as things were, than talking about themselves.

Then, as the bus moved away, Alice thought, *Poor Felix! He's going to drive all the way to Hokitika convincing himself that Camilla is just having a joke on us*. Suddenly she thought, *I hope he doesn't have an accident*, and was surprised at the sharpness of her worry for someone whom she had ceased to love.

She had time, as the bus disappeared down the narrow curving road, to realize that it was a beautiful morning. The sky was a clear and perfect blue over the luxuriant green of the bush. Through a clearing in the trees the snowpeaks were visible, and, in one incredible stream, the glacier plunged seemingly into the heart of the bush foliage. A few wisps of cloud clung around the peaks; otherwise the rain had left no sign in the shining sky.

The trees were full of movement. The soft cooing gurgling sound of wood-piegons filled the air. A black-and-white fantail flirted daintily on a branch. Webster, the tame magpie, had appeared around the side of the house and, stretching his throat, emitted a high sweet call.

"So you're going to sing to me this morning instead of give me dire warnings, are you?'' Alice said, suddenly lighthearted. It was amazing how daylight and sunshine dispelled the sinister air of the place. The clear mountain air made her want to sing with Webster and the wood-pigeons, and the chirping coquettish fantail. What a pity Camilla wasn't here to enjoy it. But Camilla had caught a plane somewhere, which to her would be much more exciting. How irritatingly mysterious she had chosen to be! Even a week ago, when she had written that note of welcome, she had made no suggestion of this dramatic development. But a week ago she couldn't have known of it, Alice thought slowly. Because she had been writing *D is so impetuous*.

Whom had she married, and why so suddenly?

''Lend it to me!'' Webster said suddenly, in the small eerie voice that was such a caricature of his lovely liquid singing notes. He strutted down the path, peering at the ground with his head on one side, muttering absorbedly, ''Lend it to me!'' He was small and restless, like someone's conscience, Alice thought. Who had been reiterating to Camilla ''Lend it to me!'' often enough for Webster to pick up the words?

And what did Camilla, who, for all her rather miserly efforts to accumulate money, had always been poor, have to lend?

Suddenly, with utter certainty, she knew it was fantastically unlikely that Camilla should have gone off secretly to get married.

A figure on a bicycle had suddenly appeared at the turn in the road. It was a girl pedaling vigorously. She was short and stout and dressed in slacks and an old blue jersey. There was a milk billy hanging on the handles of her bicycle.

"What oh!" she called to Alice. "There was no one here when I called yesterday so I didn't leave any milk. Where's Miss Mason?"

"She's not here," Alice said rather foolishly. The girl had a round, cheerful, freckled face and inquisitive eyes. She looked a precocious fifteen with a liking for scandal. Nevertheless, her face was friendly and good-natured.

"That's a pity. I've got a note for her. From Him."

She handed Alice the envelope while Alice's brain whirled. Surely this was not another man. It was too much!

"When will she be back?" the girl pursued.

"I don't quite know. Maybe not at all. But if you bring the milk I'd better have some. I'm staying here."

The girl's eyes popped.

"Why, what goes on? Has Miss Mason left? Are you the new teacher or something?"

"No, I'm not the new teacher. I've merely come to visit Camilla, but she seems to have gone off and got herself married."

"Whew!" The girl let out a low whistle. "What's He say?" The word was still spoken with emphasis.

"Hadn't you better explain?" Alice suggested.

The girl leaned on her bicycle and prepared, with enjoyment, to make her explanation.

"I'm Tottie. I work up at the farm for Mr. Dalton Thorpe and his sister." (Dalton! Another D. Was he the impetuous one?) "He's ever so handsome," Tottie went on. "She's nice, too. She was fond of Miss Mason. Often had her up there reading to her and so on. She doesn't see many people. I think she was hoping her brother would marry Miss Mason, and sure enough it looked that way. Any girl'd be crazy about him, and then there were things he gave her."

"What did he give her?" Alice asked, despising herself for gossiping with the milk girl, but feeling instinctively the thing was too important to ignore.

Tottie looked sly.

"It's not for me to tell things like that. Anyway, I've only got my suspicions. But there were hints enough. My, who was it she did marry in the end? Not that new bus driver who's been hanging around?"

Alice found herself suddenly disliking Tottie's familiarity.

"Of course it wasn't," she said tartly. "It wasn't anyone here as far as I know."

"Gosh! She was a bit of a goer, wasn't she? That is going to knock Mr. Thorpe. He'd really fallen for her, I'd say. My," she said precociously, climbing on her bicycle, "if I behaved like this with men I'd get shot."

The last statement stuck unpleasantly in Alice's mind as she went inside.

The yellow cat was following her, asking for food. Absently she poured milk out of the billy into a saucer and set it on the floor for him. While he lapped, with sudden resolution she tore open the letter Tottie had given her. She didn't excuse herself for the action. She did it on an impulse, feeling that no clue that might lead to the solution of Camilla's surprising action should be ignored.

The writing on the single sheet of paper said simply,

I've missed you so much, darling. Where have you been? Will you come over tonight?

It had no signature.

That proved Tottie's story. Whoever Dalton Thorpe was, he, too, was under Camilla's spell.

Were there no other women on the coast? Alice wondered bewilderedly. Camilla wasn't as devastating as all that. She was attractive, certainly, but silly, easily flattered, unreliable and, quite obviously, extraordinarily deceitful. It would have amused her to have three men dancing attendance on her, and no doubt she would have exploited them to the utmost, with one eye on the main chance. When the main chance had turned up from an unexpected quarter she apparently hadn't hesitated to take it.

Yet somehow Alice couldn't rid herself of the feeling that Camilla wasn't far away, and that one of these men with the initial D knew more about her whereabouts than he was saying. *D is so impetuous*. That was the clue. Alice picked up the calendar and studied the brief notes again. The thought had occurred to her that if Camilla's marriage had been unexpected (as it must have been, since she had not anticipated being away when she had answered Alice's letter) she might have made some appointments ahead. She turned the calendar leaves, and there, on the next day, was an appointment: *Dinner with Dod. Dod says he would kill me if I played fast and loose with him.*

Dod, Alice was thinking. That would be Camilla's affectionate nickname for Felix, shortening the Dodsworth to the friendly one-syllable Dod. But it made another D. It made a mysterious triangle of D's. *Dod says he would kill me. . . .*One could almost hear Felix's light careless words that silly impressionable Camilla had taken seriously. Or had they really been serious?

Felix who had said so certainly when Alice had told him of Camilla's marriage, "I don't believe it." Felix who had glibly changed an appointment with the absent Camilla to one with Alice. Felix, laughing, careless, unconcerned, secret.

No! The word screamed in Alice's head. Camilla was really legitimately married to some stranger. Her letter left on the mantelpiece was true. She had gone in a great hurry and hadn't had time to pack all her clothes or cancel her appointment with Felix. In the bedroom there were drawers ruffled untidily as if she had thrown things into a suitcase in a hurry. The wardrobe held her thick winter overcoat, and several dresses and pairs of shoes. She would send for them; she was too thrifty to leave things behind. Alice could never remember her throwing away a garment until it was mended beyond hope. Over everything there clung the odor of Camilla's perfume, carnation. It gave the uncomfortable illusion that Camilla was there, just in the next room, ready to call out in her high excited voice. There was a scrap of paper on the littered dressing-table. It was tucked under the powder bowl. Obviously it was one of Camilla's notes to jog her memory.

Get mothballs in town on Wednesday, it read.

Wednesday was the day which bore the red ring around it on the calendar, clearly the day on which Camilla had planned to do something important. The prosaic statement "Get mothballs" was utterly at odds with the wild romance of her marriage. Town would be Hokitika. Camilla had known she was going to Hokitika on Wednesday.

Had she known she was not coming back?

Suddenly the mystery of it was all too much for Alice. She was aware that she was ravenously hungry and that there was nothing in the house to eat. She would go across to Dundas Hill's and borrow some bread or invite herself to breakfast.

"I'll be back soon," she said gaily to the cat and the bird. (The cottage in the woods, with its two small inhabitants, was like something out of *Grimm's Fairy Tales.* Was there an ogre, too?) Webster hopped after her to the gate, flapping his clipped wings and saying in his small rapid voice, "Go away quick! Quick!"

"Phooey to you!" said Alice. "You old misery."

She walked quickly down the road, admiring the tall trees arching over the everlasting creeping ferns, listening for the clear beautiful notes of the black tui and the small shy bell-bird.

Around the bend of the road she came on a sign which read DUNDAS HILL. CLIMBING EQUIPMENT AND PHOTOGRAPHY. A long drive bordered on either side by masses of dahlias, drooping and shaggy from the rain, led to a tall old house set back among shiny-leaved ngaio trees and giant tree ferns. One of the large front windows of the house was made into a shop front, and as Alice drew nearer she saw that it contained skis, climbing boots and alpenstocks in the window, also a very fine display of photographs of the glacier and various snowpeaks.

In the distance, beyond the bush, she could catch a glimpse of a green valley ringed with mountain peaks, and the long rambling glacier hotel and surrounding buildings.

So the isolation she had felt in the rain last night had not been genuine. She was within a quarter of a mile of the rest of the tiny mountain settlement.

The discovery greatly increased Alice's confidence. She went past the bright shock-headed ranks of dahlias up to Dundas Hill's front door and rang the bell.

Dundas himself opened the door. He looked as if he was just dressed, his cheeks bright from shaving, his stiff straight gray hair on end. There were slight pouches under his eyes as if he hadn't slept, and his eyes themselves looked strangely colorless, like a cat's in bright sunlight. His short figure was inclined to stoutness. He gave an impression of common sense and kindness and utter dependability. Only his eyes were puzzling and set him apart from ordinariness.

"Good morning, Miss Ashton," he said warmly. "I was just going to come over and see how you had survived the night."

Alice saw no point in telling him of her imaginary fears. "I survived it very well, thank you. I've come to see if I can borrow some bread. And can you tell me where one does one's shopping here?"

"There's a store near the hotel. But you're going to have breakfast with us, of course. My daughter is getting it. Margaretta!"

"Yes," a rather sulky voice answered from somewhere within.

"Come in," Dundas said to Alice, smiling with his pleased kindness.

She followed him down a long hall to a room where a girl of about seventeen in a shabby dress that was too small for her was setting the table for breakfast. The girl turned at their entrance and Alice saw Dundas' light-colored eyes in a heavy sullen face. She was well developed for her age, with a square body like her father's. Her breasts strained against the cotton material of the outgrown frock.

"Margaretta," Dundas said, "this is Miss Alice Ashton, a friend of Camilla's. This is my daughter, Miss Ashton."

Margaretta muttered something in reply to Alice's friendly greeting and began to walk out of the room.

"Miss Ashton is having breakfast with us," Dundas told her, as if unaware of the girl's discourtesy. "Set another place."

The girl nodded and disappeared. Alice looked around the room. It contained an extraordinary conglomeration of stuff. There was far too much heavy dark furniture. One wall was entirely covered with miniatures in elaborate gilt frames. Various small tables held Satsuma and Cloisonné bowls, enameled ashtrays and pieces of crystal. The sideboard was loaded with pieces of silver that badly needed polishing, and along the high carved mantelpiece Alice suddenly saw Dundas' ladies, a dozen or so Dresden figures with tiny waists, tiny fine hands and pointed toes peeping beneath their crinolined skirts. Above them a cuckoo clock ticked sedately. The room might have been a second-rate antique shop. There was an almost magpie miscellany about it, as if nothing had ever been thrown out.

Alice sat on a period couch covered with a faded tapestry that bore a design of pink cabbage roses. She became aware of Dundas' voice.

"Is there no sign of Camilla yet?"

He asked the question politely, as if the matter of Camilla's absence were of no great moment to him. His casualness was an elaborate deception of his true feelings.

"Oh, Camilla," said Alice brightly. Here was another one who was going to grieve Camilla's passing. (Camilla's passing! How had a gloomy phrase like that come into her head?) "She's run off to be married. She left a note for me, but it slipped down and I didn't find it until after you had gone last night."

To her surprise Dundas didn't say "I don't believe it" indignantly, as Felix had. On the contrary, he nodded his head gravely, as if the news didn't surprise him.

"Do you know, I was afraid of something like that. I didn't like to say so last night, but I had a feeling something had happened. With Camilla it wouldn't be simple."

"That's true," Alice agreed. "She would want to do it the sensational way."

"She was a very naughty girl," Dundas said in his mild old-fashioned way. "In the school she kept no order. The children did as they liked. She persisted in living in that tumbledown house when we wanted it pulled down. As for the rest—"

"What was the rest?" Alice asked interestedly.

"Why, men, of course. She thought she could behave as she liked with them. She thought they were all willing to be made fools of."

Alice understood his disapproval now. He was jealous, of course. Probably he had never approved of Camilla.

"Have you any idea," she asked, "who this man she has married is?"

"Not the slightest. Though now you mention it I do recall seeing one of those big American cars at her gate the other day. No one here has an American car. It could have belonged to this stranger she seems to have run off with. I admit her behavior doesn't surprise me. I realize," he concluded wistfully, "that she didn't confide in me."

"She said something about catching a plane," Alice said. Poor Dundas—he was being awfully decent about Camilla's casual behavior. "Probably it was someone staying at the hotel. You'll have to get another teacher."

"Yes. This is really most irregular. We must have someone here when the school reopens next week. But at least now we've got the chance to have the schoolhouse demolished."

"Wait until I've spent a week in it," Alice pleaded. "I like it and I couldn't afford the hotel."

"I'm afraid—"

What he had been going to say was interrupted by Margaretta coming in with three plates of porridge.

42

She set them down and silently waited for Alice and Dundas to be seated.

Dundas came back to his paternal geniality and said, "Margaretta is getting to be a very good housekeeper. Her mother died when she was quite small, and we've had one woman after another, but now Margaretta manages herself. Don't you, dear?"

Margaretta, her head bent over her plate, did not answer. Alice looked at her badly brushed hair curling on the tender pale nape of her neck. Poor kid, it was a shame the way she was dressed. Her father, she thought, was not a man to notice clothes, but didn't she care herself?

Dundas' gaze was wandering around the room.

"I've kept everything the way it was since my wife died, except for a few little additional things I have got. The miniatures and the Dresden ladies are mine. I confess I love small things." He curved his fingers as if he were imagining them around one of the slender china waists. "It's just a foolish idiosyncrasy of mine. But most of the other things were my wife's. I'm too sentimental. But we like it, don't we, Margaretta?"

Again the girl made no response. Dundas leaned over to a small table to pick up an enameled snuffbox.

"My wife brought most of these from England. She was English, you know. She had no relatives in New Zealand." He held the box up to the light and blew on it gently. "A little dust, pet," he murmured. "But your father's too fussy, isn't he? And this piece is Satsuma. Not particularly valuable, but the colors are good." He revolved a shining blue bowl in his hands. "And this little one is French enamel. As a collection there's not very much, but I value it. You must see my studio and my darkroom, Miss Ashton. Margaretta helps me with the printing and developing."

Alice tried to talk to the downbent head.

"That must be interesting, Margaretta."

Her only response was an ambiguous movement of the head. It was clear that Margaretta was not going to be drawn out just then. She was very rude, but she was at a difficult age, when nothing was simple, when one's loves or hates were extravagant and exhausting. It seemed that Margaretta might hate the cluttered room, with its museum-like atmosphere. It was a great pity about her clothes. An attractive dress might do a lot for her.

Thinking of clothes, Alice began to chatter.

"Camilla left practically all her things in the house. I wonder what I should do with them."

"She'll send for them, I should think."

"Yes. I expect so. She's much too thrifty just to discard them. I had a glance through her stuff, but the only interesting thing I found was the calendar."

Dundas looked up.

"The calendar?"

"Camilla has a shocking memory," Alice explained. "She always jots things down. She'd been doing it on one of those desk calendar things where there's a leaf for every day." Something prompted her to add, "It's quite illuminating. That, and Webster's chatter. Webster's an amazing creature—he talks like a parrot. Actually better than any parrot

I've heard." Abruptly she stopped chattering as she became aware of Dundas' peculiarly colorless gaze. His eyes were like clear water.

"What particular things were on the calendar?" (*Why, he's got a guilty conscience, poor sweet,* Alice reflected amusedly.)

"Oh, this and that. People. Things she was going to do. I shall keep it to tease her with."

"I'd like to have a look at it," Dundas said. "It might give a clue as to her whereabouts. The man—"

"Oh, there isn't only one man in it," Alice said flippantly. "All the same, you know, I hardly think Camilla would want them all reading her private comments." Suddenly, with his tense gaze on her, she was sorry for her urge to tease him. "She *was* naughty, you know," she said gently. "I think perhaps it's a good thing she's gone."

Dundas breathed heavily.

"Perhaps it is. But we were fond of Camilla, in spite of her faults. All of us. In fairness to her, if you don't wish that diary to be read, I think it should be burnt."

"I agree," said Alice. "But later. When we're quite sure—"

"Sure of what?"

"That Camilla's all right. Just at present there *may* be occasion to refer to that diary."

Dundas' clear colorless gaze never left her.

"You think so? In what way, Miss Ashton?"

"Well—in case this elopement of hers is a hoax."

"I hardly think that would be so. At this stage I almost hope not. For the sake of the school I wouldn't like any more scandal." He paused, to add perplexedly, "Fancy your thinking something like that. But why?"

"Who is this mysterious Dalton Thorpe?" Alice asked.

Dundas seemed to welcome the change in the conversation.

"He's the owner of Glacier Farm. He's reputed to be quite wealthy. He lives alone with his sister. They lead a very quiet life. One scarcely sees them at all. He's the most eligible bachelor around, I should think." He paused. Then he said, "As far as I know Camilla was almost their only visitor."

"As far as Camilla is concerned that would be only to be expected. She has a nose for eligibility. But if it comes to that, you're an eligible person too."

"Me! Oh, I'm only a dull old widower."

"Ah, now, you're too modest. You haven't read Camilla's diary."

His color heightened; his eyes had their look of deep embarrassment.

"I think you're teasing me, Miss Ashton." Determinedly he changed the conversation. "Tell me, do you come from the same place as Camilla?"

"Yes. We went to the same school. Poor old Cam didn't have much of a time. She had no family, you know. Only an old cousin, or something. And she was as poor as a churchmouse. There was just enough money to get her educated and then she had to work. I'm glad she's got a husband now. I do hope he's good to her."

"And you?" Dundas said in his deep soft voice. "You have a family?"

Suddenly Alice was thinking of Camilla's lack of

family. There had been that dreary old Cousin Maud with whom she had had to spend her holidays and whom she cordially disliked. There had been a dark parlor with several dusty pot plants in it, Alice remembered. One had always been nervous of spiders. And at nine o'clock each night Cousin Maud used to say in her thin dry voice, "Bedtime for growing girls, Camilla," and Camilla, who at sixteen had been more clever than an Indian at slithering out of the school dormitory, had had to march upstairs to the little bedroom next to Cousin Maud's and resign herself to a long dull night. When she had got her first job, with its consequent financial freedom, she had escaped from Cousin Maud's dominance. There had been little regret, Alice imagined, on either side. She remembered a letter of Camilla's: "Cousin Maud is so thankful that she has done her duty by me that now she can wash her hands of me with the greatest of pleasure. I pray we never meet again!"

So Cousin Maud would not be likely to be interested in Camilla's runaway marriage or make inquiries about her disappearance. It came to Alice with a feeling of shock that this state of affairs may have been very convenient to someone. Very convenient indeed. . . .

Something made her gaily improvise information that would be spread over the valley.

"Oh yes, I have six brothers. Isn't it crazy? We fight like anything, but I love every one of them." She grinned. "That's why I'm tough. I've been brought up the hard way. That's why I'm not frightened to stay here alone."

"Frightened?" Dundas queried. He put out his

hand to touch her arm. "But there isn't anything to be frightened of, surely. I'll come over this evening and help to pack Camilla's things. Today, as it's fine, I have an appointment with a party on the glacier to take photographs. But I'll come this evening. Promise not to touch anything until then."

He seemed so earnest that Alice was on the verge of promising, when the girl Margaretta lifted her head to look fully at Alice for the first time. Her eyes had lost their sullenness and were bright with malice.

"Don't stop Daddy, Miss Ashton. He would enjoy it. He enjoys women's clothes." Then, as if she were overcome with fright for what she had said, she picked up her empty porridge plate and rushed out of the room.

IV

WHEN ALICE RETURNED to the cottage there was a smart cream-and-red car drawn up at the gate.

Alice's heart gave a great leap. Camilla was back. This must be the American car Dundas had spoken about. Camilla was back with her new husband and everything was all right.

She ran up the path and burst inside.

"Hi! Camilla! And it's just about time!"

There was no answer at all.

"Hi!" said Alice again, uncertainty creeping into her voice. "Who's there?"

She heard a slight movement in Camilla's bedroom and, a little nervous now, went to the door.

The girl was crouching on the floor. She had one of Camilla's nightgowns in her hands, and her eyes were raised expectantly, almost fearfully. She was one of the loveliest women Alice had ever seen.

It was partly her surprise, partly her genuine admiration for the apple-blossom skin, the soft dark hair and the wide-open brilliant blue eyes that made Alice unable to speak.

As she stared the girl got slowly to her feet, still clutching the nightgown, saying in a scared voice, "I'm sorry. I wasn't stealing. I only came to find Camilla. Tottie said she had gone, but I didn't believe her."

Alice knew now who she must be. The Thorpe girl, Dalton Thorpe's sister. But no one had prepared her for that extraordinary beauty.

"She really has gone," Alice said. "I wouldn't have believed it either, only there was the letter."

"But she's left all her things!" the girl said. Her enormous blue eyes, dominating her small perfect face, were full of bewilderment. "She *couldn't* have gone like that, without saying good-bye. And who are you, anyway? What are you doing here?"

"I'm Alice Ashton, a friend of Camilla's. I've come to stay"—Alice flung out her hands in humorous friendliness, because the girl seemed so queerly shy and frightened—"and here I find I have no hostess."

"I'm Katherine Thorpe," the girl said. "Perhaps you've guessed. Perhaps Camilla has written to you about me."

"Camilla was no letter-writer," Alice explained. "And I haven't been back in New Zealand long. But I have heard about you and your brother. As a matter of fact that's where we thought Camilla was."

"We?"

"Oh, just Felix Dodsworth and I. He's driving the bus. We were old friends. He said he thought Camilla might have spent the night with you because it was raining so hard."

"Yes, she's done that often," Katherine Thorpe

said eagerly. "We used to persuade her to, Dalton and I. We don't see many people; in fact I see scarcely any at all. Dalton almost keeps me like a prisoner. But we liked Camilla. She was so bright." The girl's eyelids drooped. "Dalton liked her very much indeed," she said primly.

"I know. It's all in the diary." Again Alice was exaggerating the contents of that diary. Some instinct was making her do so to see what reaction she got.

"The diary?"

"A funny sort of diary. Rather indiscreet. Camilla liked men, you know."

"Men? Other ones than Dalton?"

Really, the girl's innocence was only equaled by her extraordinary looks. That brother of hers must have kept her in a convent. Couldn't she have seen Camilla's honeybee tendencies?

"Well—there must have been, mustn't there, since she has married one of them."

"I truly can't believe that," said Katherine, almost pathetically. "She would have told me. She was my best friend, the only friend I have."

Her blue eyes misted and threatened to swim in enormous tears.

"I'll show you her letter," Alice said hurriedly.

She went to the kitchen to get it. (Was it really Camilla's letter? It was printed. Anyone could print rather than imitate handwriting.)

When Katherine had perused it with close attention, she abruptly crumpled the sheet of paper up and the threatened tears came.

"Then it is true! Oh, how unkind! Poor Dalton! He

loved her, you know. I think he was going to marry her. Oh, how can I tell him this? How could she *be* so unkind?''

Running away, Alice thought cynically, seemed to be the first prudent thing Camilla had done. She could scarcely have untangled her complicated affairs had she remained here.

Then suddenly Katherine said, ''I don't believe she has gone away, because why would she leave all her things? Look! Here's the nightdress she wore the last time she stayed at our place. She was very pleased with it. She had made it herself.'' She held up the filmy blue garment she had been clutching. ''That's too good to leave behind. And all her own things here. It wouldn't be sensible to leave them.''

''It looks as if she went in rather a hurry,'' Alice said uneasily. ''We expect her to send for her things in a day or so. Then we'll know where she is.''

''Of course, one can't take much on a plane,'' Katherine said. ''I expect it is true then. She must have gone.''

Her lovely sensitive mouth began to droop again. She sniffed like a child. Miserably she looked at Alice.

''You must think I'm a baby. But it's so lonely here. Camilla was bright. She cheered me up. I'll miss her frightfully. As for poor Dalton—'' She shook her head. ''Well, I must go. Dalton will be annoyed with me for taking the car out alone. I'm just learning to drive and he never lets me out alone. You're not angry with me for coming snooping like this, are you?''

"Of course I'm not angry."

Was this incredibly lovely person just a little neurotic? She had long, narrow, very thin hands, with knucklebones that protruded sharply. Now she had dropped the nightgown she kept her hands clutched together. She was either very nervous or very distressed. When she suddenly said, "You have pretty hair. It's prettier than Camilla's really. Camilla's was a little coarse. Would you come over and visit us one day?" Alice had a feeling that Katherine was going to lay her thin sharply boned fingers on her hair and smooth it. She was a beautiful-looking girl, but there was something about her hands or the brilliance of her great eyes that was oddly disturbing. Yet she had been Camilla's friend, and if one was to find out what had led Camilla to her surprising actions one had to get to know all her friends, to do what Camilla had done, to wear her mantle—of trouble, or danger, or whatever other complicated atmosphere it carried.

She moved a little away from her visitor and said politely, "Why, of course. I'd be glad to come."

Katherine smiled.

"How nice. Not tomorrow. Everyone here dines at the hotel on Saturday night. It's just a custom. Rather a boring one, but it's the only time Dalton ever takes me out. What about Sunday for tea?"

After she had gone Alice began to tidy up the odd clothes of Camilla's that she had strewn about the room in her bewilderment. It was then that she discovered, at the back of a drawer filled with old letters, exercise books, magazines and sundry jars of face cream, unmended stockings and handkerchiefs, the other loose-leaf calendar, last year's, with its inevitable Camilla comments.

Sitting on the floor in the small dark room that always, because of the encroaching bush, swam in a green gloom, Alice turned page after page of the block, and read the various inane and unimportant comments that dated from Camilla's arrival six months ago. Only the more significant ones registered in her mind:

July 4th. Go to Thorpe farm. Wonder what the brother is like.

July 18th. Don't forget eleven o'clock for glacier. Dundas always wanting to photograph me, such a bore. And the later comment in brackets: (*Was terrified, even with Dundas looking after me. Wonder if it's true what they say. Poor darling, he's so sweet.*)

July 20th. Dalton Thorpe absolutely thrilling—he makes me think of Rudolph Valentino.

August 8th. Margaretta such a dull child. They say she adores her father.

A month later she was writing, *Hokitika (hair net, nylons, face powder, new history books).* Then the added comment obviously made on her return. *New bus driver, Felix Dodsworth. He doesn't look a bit like a bus driver. I shall call him Dod. Nice having a new man about.*

On the fourteenth of November there was a cryptic entry, *Gosh, what a present!*

Then a mysterious one, *Answer solicitor's letter.*

Then, at the beginning of December, *Can't get away for holidays. Things here becoming too interesting.*

And three weeks later, *Good news, Alice is going to come. Can ask her advice.*

But a day later she was writing, in agitation, if the wavering scrawl was any indication of her state of mind, *D won't wait.*

Then, on the last day of the year, with great firmness, she had made the comment, *Tomorrow New Year—will have to straighten things out. It might be fun, but it's getting a bit dangerous. Perhaps I had better listen to D.*

The calendar clasped in her hands, Alice sat back on her heels. The little room with its odor of carnation seemed uncannily still. One might be a goldfish in a green bowl swimming around and around, never arriving anywhere. Which was a good thing, because one didn't quite care to arrive at any place or any conclusion to one's startled thoughts.

To reassure herself, Alice got out writing materials and began a letter to Camilla:

You untidy little wretch, why do you always leave so many loose ends in your life? Here I am with them flapping all around me. You might think it amusing to go off and leave three men pining for you—I suppose now you have got the fourth (who is he, darling?) you don't give a snap of your fingers for the three D's. But I assure you it isn't all fun for me.

Why did you have that irritating habit of referring to them all by their initial in your diary? Now I don't know where I am because I never know whom you mean. Who is the impetuous one? Who is the impatient one? Why were things getting dangerous? Seriously, you must tell me, because it looks as if your mantle (and a troubled one) has fallen on me, and I shall have to cope with these three indignant swains.

Honestly, darling, what made you go off in such a mad rush and leave everything? I am packing your clothes and will send them on to you when you let me know where you are. I have gone through your drawers—just as if you were dead, it's really a bit grim—but there's a tin trunk I can't find the key to. I expect I'll find it in one of your funny unlikely places.

I have adopted your orphan family. The cat is beautiful, but Webster makes me intensely uncomfortable. I keep thinking he is my conscience—or yours! Only you haven't got one, have you, darling?

Much against Dundas' wish (he seems desperately anxious to burn down the house, and I admit it is a disgrace to a self-respecting school committee), I am staying here until I have been on the glacier and done all the tourist things. I can't afford to stay at the hotel, anyway. This is my holiday, and I intend to make the most of it in spite of your defection.

Where the devil *are* you? The bathroom stinks of that awful carnation soap you use, and I expect you to walk in any minute. I can't get over the feeling that you are much closer than we think. . . .

Now she was just writing her thoughts, overcome

by the deep disturbing conviction that this letter would never be posted.

What was in that locked trunk? Suddenly she felt it absolutely imperative to know. The lock was old and rusty. She could probably break it with a poker.

After ten minutes of strenuous effort the lock fell to pieces. As Alice's hands were on the lid of the trunk she was aware that it had begun to rain again. The mantle of clouds had settled down over the house like Camilla's mantle of trouble on her own shoulders. The room was almost dark. The rain on the roof brought back her feeling of floating breathlessly under water, cool, dark, green water that had no surface. All the intensity of her apprehension was back. She could scarcely bring herself to raise the lid of the trunk.

That was silly, silly! It would just be full of more of Camilla's hoarded rubbish. She and Dundas were a good pair. An odor of mothballs came out as Alice's determined hands raised the lid. There were layers of tissue paper. (It wasn't a body, anyway. No one ever wrapped a body in tissue paper and mothballs.) Probably it was a treasured evening gown.

But no. As Alice ripped away the last layer of tissue paper she saw the beautiful gray squirrel coat lying there.

Get mothballs in town today. The words were so insistent that they might have been spoken.

Camilla had wanted the mothballs to pack with the coat. She had intended bringing them back.

But she hadn't come back.

Now Alice, like Felix, no longer believed the story

of Camilla's marriage. It was no longer possible to believe it.

Because she knew Camilla too well. She knew that never in her life could she bring herself to leave behind her so lovely and valuable a coat as this.

V

FOR THE SECOND TIME since her arrival Alice noticed the keas. Three of them had been perched on the roof of the bus which had just arrived and stood outside the hotel and had been picking with their sharp inquisitive beaks at the luggage and packages. When the swinging doors of the hotel opened and some people came out talking loudly they swept into the air, screeching their anger. The underside of their wings was a rich fantasy of color: emerald green, blue, blood red—a brilliant nightmare it must seem to the stricken eyes of the lambs on which they preyed. One perched on a windowsill, folding its wings drably, and regarding Alice with its inquisitive, baleful and treacherous eye. The peculiar foreboding she had felt on her arrival swept over her again. For no reason she had developed an anathema to those squat, noisy mountain birds.

She hesitated on the doorstep of the hotel, all the lively courage she had felt while dressing in the little schoolhouse leaving her.

There, she had stood in front of the mirror saying, "Sorry, Camilla. Sorry, darling. I know how jealous you are of your clothes. But I have to do this. It's for your sake."

Webster had hopped onto the end of the bed and stood looking at her with his head on one side.

"Well, encyclopedia, what do you think?" Alice had asked.

"Nevermore," said Webster in his small harsh croak.

"I should think not," said Alice severely. "I almost have an idea Camilla echoes you. Nevermore, indeed!"

She tucked the lapels of the coat under her chin. It was a little too big for her. She felt wrapped in a soft gray cocoon. But Camilla was taller. The well-cut swinging back and the rolled collar must have looked wonderful on her. Camilla must have reveled in it. It wasn't, as fur coats went, a highly expensive kind. For instance, it was but a poor relation of her mother's mink and chinchilla. But to Camilla, who had had to count every penny and who had always made all her own clothes, the three hundred pounds or so that this would have cost must have seemed fabulous for one garment. So that it was all the more perplexing that she should have left it behind.

Would the experiment tonight solve anything? Alice held her little head high and longed for more inches. If she could look at the mysterious Dalton Thorpe, at kind Dundas and at laughing secretive Felix from their own level she would not be afraid at all. Of course, she was not afraid of Dundas, who was shy, nor of Felix, whom she thought she knew so well, nor of any man. It was only this intangible something, this apprehension that crept up on one out of the rain and the wet green bush and the low mist. And the sweet carnation odor that reminded one incessantly of Camilla's absence.

Would tonight prove anything? Alice struck a pose and declaimed *Look like the innocent flower, but be the serpent under't* to her fur-clad image in the mirror.

"Nevermore," muttered Webster.

Alice giggled at the absurdity of the uncanny creature's comments and her apprehension left her.

But now it was back again as she forced herself to push open the swinging doors of the hotel and walk through the brightly lit lobby into the lounge.

Nothing happened at all. She sat down and beckoned to a waiter and primly ordered a sherry. Then she eased the coat off her shoulders and looked about her. The guests were the conventional tourist type. Most of them were sunburnt and peeling. There was some loud chatter about strained muscles and ice crevasses and scree slopes. One or two of the younger men glanced towards her curiously, thinking her a new arrival. The lounge was large and raftered, with a huge fireplace, and decorated with pictures of mountain peaks and bowls of immense raupo heads and toi-toi plumes. Alice could hear the harsh impatient screech of the keas outside. It was beginning to rain again, too, the thin mist of it webbing against the wall of bush. But in here all was warmth and cheer and lightheartedness.

Then Dundas and Margaretta came in. Margaretta came through the door first, but immediately she slipped behind her father as if trying to efface herself as she crossed the room. She was a tall girl, with strong well-formed limbs. When she learned to walk with grace and confidence she might, almost, in spite of her heavy brows and sullen jaw, be handsome. Alice wondered if it was from a desire to look smaller and slimmer that Margaretta wore clothes too small for her. Tonight she had on a brown velvet that might have been her party dress two years ago. Her hair was done in two thick plaits and pinned around her head. She was a curious mixture of child and grownup. She looked intensely unhappy, so unhappy that something must have happened very recently to cause it.

Looking for somewhere to sit, Dundas suddenly saw her and his face lighted with pleasure.

"Miss Ashton! I was going to suggest this, but I was afraid you might think it presumptuous."

Dundas, with his over-polite language that somehow was out of tune with his broad shoulders and thick-set body, and with his dowdy young daughter.

"Oh, I shouldn't have thought that," Alice answered. "Hullo, Margaretta. Are you going to sit with me?"

"If we may," said Dundas with alacrity. "What are you drinking? Let's have another."

Alice unostentatiously pulled the coat out of the way and patted the couch for Margaretta to sit down.

The girl did so, and Dundas beckoned a waiter.

"Is yours sherry, Miss Ashton? Three sherries, please. We'll be grownup tonight, eh, Margaretta?"

Alice said, "Oh, doesn't Margaretta usually have sherry?"

"Well—she's never particularly wanted it. Have you, dear? Actually she's young for her age, for which I am very glad. I have no wish to lose her for a long time." He laid his hand affectionately on his daughter's shoulder. "It astonished me when she had a young swain who wanted her to go dancing tonight."

"Why didn't you go?" Alice asked Margaretta.

The waiter had come with the drinks, and while Dundas was paying for them Margaretta said violently, under her breath. "How could I, with nothing to wear?"

But the next moment she was taking the glass of sherry from her father and looking her usual silent self.

Before Alice could make any further comment there was a stir at the door and every head in the lounge was turned to see Katherine Thorpe in a dark red dress followed by a very tall man come in. Alice realized that Katherine would cause this stir of interest wherever she went. Unlike poor Margaretta, whose father obviously didn't want her to grow up, Katherine was dressed like a treasured woman. The man behind her was handsome in a dark medieval way, his face narrow and pale, his expression somber. Alice remembered Camilla's excited notes—*like Rudolph Valentino*—and understood what she meant. It was indeed remarkable that neither Dalton nor his sister had married.

She leaned forward impulsively to Dundas.

"I've met Miss Thorpe, but I'd like to meet her brother. Will you introduce me?"

"Certainly," said Dundas in his polite way.

He crossed the lounge and brought the brother and sister over. Alice's heart was beating violently, not because, suddenly, she was shaking hands with this dark enigmatic-looking man (*He looks bad-tempered,* she thought involuntarily), but because of what, presently, she meant to do.

She heard Katherine Thorpe saying in her high excitable voice, "Oh, we've met already. Alice is coming to visit us, Dalton."

She thought Dalton frowned; it was difficult to know, for his brows were perpetually slightly drawn together. She felt instinctively that he didn't like visitors, perhaps particularly women. Or perhaps because, in a way, she was a successor to Camilla. Camilla's chatter had probably amused him and drawn him out. Silent men often liked talkative women. Perhaps his somber look now was because he was deeply upset by Camilla's faithlessness.

"Oh, yes," he said stiffly, and Dundas broke into the awkward pause by saying in his affable voice, "What will you have to drink, Miss Thorpe?"

At that moment Alice's breath caught. Then she controlled it and said with perfect calm, "There's our bus driver, Mr. Dodsworth."

(Felix, I'm not going through the rest of my life losing my breath when I see you. It's purely reflex now. Or if it isn't you'll just have to keep out of my sight.)

Dundas turned.

"Ah, yes. He's not really a bus driver, you know. He's an actor of some repute, according to Camilla. A most entertaining fellow. They treat him as a guest

64

here. Shall we ask him to have a drink?"

Katherine turned and her brilliant eyes rested on Felix.

"Oh, do," she said warmly.

Dalton's scowl seemed to deepen. He laid his hand on her arm and seemed about to say something. Then he refrained, and Dundas was beckoning Felix over.

Felix's lively smile enveloped them all. He said, "Hi, Alice. Hi, Margaretta." But over his introduction to Katherine Thorpe he lingered and his eyes swept warmly over her. Alice knew that look so well. She used to deceive herself that it was an assessing one, when he was looking for new talent, but now she knew better. It was simply frank appreciation and admiration for a beautiful woman.

Suddenly it was easy to do what she had meant to because it took her mind off Felix. They all had drinks now, and Alice held hers up, saying brightly, "Why don't we all drink to Camilla? We ought to wish her happiness."

Was there the smallest hesitation? It was Felix who responded almost at once in his lighthearted deceptive way, "That's a splendid idea." He lifted his glass. "Happiness and long life to Camilla."

With gravity the others clinked their glasses. Now their well-bred faces betrayed nothing.

"Long may she go on breaking men's hearts," Felix went on irrepressibly. His gaiety was not forced, because now there was another beautiful woman at his side. ("Why haven't I met you before?" he would be asking Katherine presently, his warm ardent eyes looking deeply into hers.)

Alice got to her feet. She picked up the fur coat and pulled it ostentatiously over her shoulders.

"Though personally," she said conversationally, "I don't think Camilla's far away, because she would never leave a coat like this behind."

Now she had everyone's startled attention. She turned, displaying the coat fully.

"It's beautiful, isn't it?" she said. "It must be quite the nicest thing old Cam's ever had. So why would she go away and leave it? It was packed so carefully in a chest. At first I thought there was a body in it, but—"

She stopped as Katherine Thorpe, who had gone very white, groped her way backwards to a chair.

"What are you suggesting?" she asked in a whisper.

Alice sat down again slowly. She was aware that Margaretta looked frightened, too, her mouth hanging slightly open, her sturdy hands clenched, her eyes shocked. But most of all she was aware of the three men standing in a half-circle, Camilla's three D's: Dundas with his colorless eyes suddenly all black pupil like a cat's at night; Dalton's narrow face having a fierce controlled look as if there were dark anger or fear welling inside him; Felix's brows drawn down in one of their storms of impatience, the way they used to when someone overplayed or behaved without intelligence.

Suddenly she knew what the three men were like: the squat alert-eyed keas; and they, trembling Katherine, Margaretta in her hot childish dress, and herself, foolish and impulsive and not very brave, were the defenseless lambs.

And Camilla had been a lamb, too—Camilla, who

had fled leaving all her possessions, even her beautiful new coat.

Fled?

The queer tense silence was broken by Dalton Thorpe saying, "That does seem rather odd, I admit. But I know nothing about Camilla's so-called elopement." His voice was dry. "I was not in on the secret."

"It appears none of us were," said Felix with his irrepressible cheerfulness.

Dundas said seriously, "It's all most irregular, as far as her job goes. School reopens next week. She might have thought of that."

(How odd it was, Alice thought, that Camilla hadn't left a note for Dundas as well as for her. She had always taken work lightly, but not with such irresponsible lightness as that.)

Katherine Thorpe leaned forward to Alice. Now there were two red spots of color in her cheeks.

"Why are you wearing that coat?" she hissed.

"I've just borrowed it," Alice said. "Camilla never minded my borrowing her things."

"I believe you know something about her. After all, how did you happen to arrive on the spot just at this time?"

Dalton moved forward. His face was thin and dark.

"Katherine!"

Katherine's face changed curiously. She looked for a moment as if she were going to weep. Then a blank look came over her face and she murmured something inaudible.

Dalton said, "My sister's upset. She was very fond of Camilla."

"She was my best friend," Katherine whispered.

"Not was," said Dundas in his brisk normal voice. "You're using the wrong tense, Miss Thorpe. I have no doubt Camilla will be back to regale us with her sins! Eh?" He gave his mild pleasant laugh. "She'll be back for that coat, anyway. So what are we worrying about?"

Margaretta made a slight movement. Her eyes were on her father. She had a slightly hypnotized look; was it like a frightened rabbit? But what could be frightening Margaretta? What could be frightening Katherine? If it came to that, no one was completely undisturbed. Even Dundas, striving to restore normality, had perspiration on his brow.

Yet afterwards it all seemed like a damp squib. The tension had lasted only a few moments while each man wondered how Camilla had come to deceive him. Indeed, one wondered if there had been tension at all, apart from Katherine Thorpe's nervous excitability. Dundas, in his efficient way, had arranged that they all eat together, and dinner had been a pleasant if not hilarious meal. After dinner dancing started in the lounge.

Alice said, "What fun!" and Katherine turned animatedly to her brother and cried almost pleadingly, as if she anticipated a certain refusal, "Oh, do let's stay, Dalton. They hardly ever have enough young people here to start a dance. It will be fun for Margaretta. Oh, I'm afraid she couldn't dance in those shoes."

Everyone looked at the stout shabby brogues that made Margaretta's feet look a great deal larger and clumsier than they need have been.

Margaretta flushed painfully. "It's all right. I don't care for dancing."

Alice, suffering the girl's embarrassment with her, at the same time wanted to shake her for her defeatist attitude. What was wrong with her? She had a face as dark as the eternal clouds over those Antipodean mountains of hers.

"Margaretta, that's unnatural! Of course you like dancing. You can meet that boy who wanted you to dance with him. Look, why don't we go home and change your shoes?"

"That's a wonderful idea," said Katherine eagerly. "And I'll lend you my scarf." She took off the filmy chiffon scarf studded with brilliants that had floated loosely around her head. "We'll fluff your hair out a little. It will look so pretty."

"I've said I don't care about dancing," Margaretta muttered sulkily.

Her father came up to her.

"You go, my dear. Alice and Katherine are being very kind. Do as they tell you. Sad as it is, I am suddenly realizing you have to grow up." He opened and closed his hands slowly. "She has no mother," he said to no one in particular.

"We'll take the car," said Katherine gaily. "You men can have a drink while we're gone."

In the car Margaretta said explosively, "It's not Daddy's fault my clothes are shabby. There isn't any money in photography now. We have to be careful."

She didn't speak again until she had reluctantly taken them upstairs to the austere little room where she slept. In comparison with the junk-filled rooms downstairs it was like a cell.

It came to Alice that probably Margaretta preferred the austerity.

Katherine was looking about her with wide-eyed

interest. But she made no comment on the bare shabby room.

"Make-up," she said. She took Margaretta by the shoulders and pushed her onto the stool before the mirror. There were brilliant spots of color in her cheeks. She looked as if she was having tremendous fun. "You sit there while Alice brushes your hair. We're going to make you the belle of the ball. Don't look so glum, darling. You're not going to be murdered. Honestly, a man has no idea. Your father's sweet but he's just blind to what a girl needs. And you can't be that poor. Now where do you keep your shoes?

Margaretta started up. She was biting her lip and looked so distressed that Alice could see she regretted ever letting the two of them upstairs to her room.

"No, don't you get up," Katherine ordered in her imperative voice. "Alice is to do your hair. Just tell me where they are."

Almost as if in a trance Margaretta answered, "In the cupboard in the next room. The white cupboard."

Katherine went out, and Alice began to brush Margaretta's long thick hair. She could see her own head in the mirror above Margaretta's. Her fair curls were tied jauntily on top of her head with a blue ribbon. Her face, pointed-chinned, animated, looked a much younger seventeen than Margaretta's.

"Just confess you would like to meet this boy tonight and have fun," she said. "Your father does try to keep you a child, and it's wrong. How old are you really, Margaretta?"

"Eighteen. Daddy forgets. I tell him, but—" Margaretta broke off, and, fixing her hostile eyes on Alice's reflection in the mirror, she said rudely, "It's none of your business, anyway. Why do you go on staying here?"

"Why, because I like it," Alice said in surprise.

"You came to see Camilla and she isn't here. So there's no point in your staying, is there?"

"But I like it, I told you," Alice answered equably.

"But you don't know—" Margaretta began, her face suddenly crimson with some emotion. She stopped suddenly, and her square hands moved up and down her hips. The palms of them would be damp, Alice thought; and suddenly for no reason she was remembering the perspiration on Dundas' brow when they had all been looking at the fur coat.

"I can't find anything suitable," came Katherine's high voice from the next room.

"Don't know what?" Alice asked Margaretta.

"Nothing," Margaretta muttered. "But you should go away."

"Gracious!" came Katherine's voice again, on a surprised note. "Gracious, what *hoarders* you people are!"

"I haven't the faintest idea why you say that, Margaretta," Alice went on. "Don't you realize we have to be friends, Katherine and you and me, because I have a hunch it will be us who really find out what happened to Camilla, whether she's safely married or not. We have no ulterior motives like men have. And Camilla was a scamp with men. But she was good to me when I was a new kid at school and I'll never forget that. So I must be sure she's all right before I go away."

All Margaretta's response to that was her reiterated, "You oughtn't stay."

"Give me one reason," Alice said practically.

"My father likes women like you. Small."

The unexpected answer, almost wrung out of the girl, was so quaint and pathetic that Alice was both relieved and sympathetic. Poor kid! She was filled with no more complicated emotion than jealousy.

Before she could make any answer, however, Katherine had burst into the room carrying a pair of high-heeled black suède shoes.

"There was just nothing suitable in that white cupboard," she said. "You ought to make your father buy you some new shoes, darling. But I found these in the bottom of that old wardrobe. My, what a lot of clothes in there. But they're frightfully out of date. Did they belong to your mother?"

Margaretta nodded. Her eyes were fixed on the shoes in Katherine's hands.

"If you were good at sewing you could alter some of them, I'm sure. Although I do think clothes kept for years are dreary, almost a bit haunted. Were these shoes your mother's, too? See if they fit."

Margaretta put out her foot as if in a dream. For all her height she had slender feet and the black shoes fit perfectly.

"Cinderella!" Alice cried. "That's grand. Look at her hair, Katherine. It's really lovely, isn't it? With that scarf of yours—"

"And some lipstick," said Katherine eagerly. "The men just won't know her."

Margaretta was now utterly silent. She sat like a doll being dressed up. Alice was conscious of two things: that Katherine's lovely face had exactly the eager childish look of a small girl dressing her doll, and that those shoes on Margaretta's feet were somehow too modern, too new. . . . Shouldn't they have been dusty and dingy if they were several years old?

Margaretta herself kept looking uneasily at her feet. Then suddenly, just as Katherine had given her face a last triumphant dab of powder, she burst out crying.

"I don't want to go. I won't go. You're just enjoying humiliating me."

The tears ran down her face, ruining her make-up. Nothing would calm her. She kicked the shoes off her feet and stormed at them. "Go away and leave me! I won't be treated like a child! It's ridiculous. You're worse than Daddy. I wish you'd go away."

Finally they had to leave her and go back to the hotel. The three men were waiting for them, but now nobody wanted to dance.

Katherine said listlessly, "Let's go home, Dalton. I'm tired."

It seemed that her brother was relieved to take her, and it seemed that Dundas, too, was anxious to go home. But that would be because of his strange stormy daughter. He tucked his hand inside Alice's arm and said, "It was good of you to do that for Margaretta. But she's a touchy creature. She probably got stage-fright about this boy, too. She's very shy."

"It was something about the shoes," Alice said, almost to herself. "Had they an association?"

"Shoes?" said Dundas. Suddenly he exclaimed, "Black suède shoes? High heels?"

"Yes."

"Oh, but they are Camilla's. She left them one night last week when it was raining cats and dogs and wore Margaretta's gum-boots. I'll have them packed with the rest of her stuff."

Alice stared at him.

"Then why on earth didn't Margaretta say so?"

Dundas laughed. "I think between you and Katherine, such a pair of beautiful girls, you had the child tongue-tied." He patted her arm gently. "If Margaretta doesn't appreciate you, I do."

One couldn't doubt his sincerity. Already Alice liked and admired this rather odd, kind little man very much.

But she was glad that it was Felix who took her arm in a proprietary manner and said that it was time he was taking her home.

"*Thou wretched rash intruding fool!*" he said, when they got outside.

"Why?" Alice asked innocently.

"If you think there's any queer business going on you don't fling down the gauntlet like that. You watch and say nothing."

Alice was a little startled. The night was very dark, and the trees overhanging the road seemed to press in on them, making the air breathless. At the same time she was glad for this discussion with Felix, for surely it showed his innocence. Instinctively she moved closer to him.

"You mean about the fur coat?" she said. "Then you do think there is something going on."

"I don't know. Camilla was fond of animals. I can't

think she would leave them to starve."

"She meant to come back. I'm sure she did. Something's happened to stop her." Somehow her mind shied away from what that something might be. She added, "Dundas had seen an American car at the cottage once or twice."

"Had he?" said Felix, with interest. "Then what a secretive little devil she is."

"She'll write and explain," Alice said. "But honestly, it puzzles me how Camilla had all you men on a string. She's such an empty little creature, really. And that, believe me, isn't said from jealousy."

"I'm not on a string," said Felix in his light careless voice. "Not me."

Alice was going to protest, then remembered that tonight Felix had seen Katherine Thorpe for the first time. Naturally he had slipped off Camilla's string. He must, indeed, be thankful for Camilla's disappearing act. Poor susceptible Felix, who wasn't empty like Camilla at all, but who had all of that young lady's tendency to a roving eye.

"Anyway," said Alice, "I shall find it interesting visiting the Thorpes tomorrow. He seems a Heathcliff kind of person. I shouldn't be at all surprised if he knows more than anyone what has happened to Camilla. But Katherine's perfectly lovely. Isn't she?"

She made her question on a light upward inflexion, as if she cared nothing for Felix's reply.

He surprised her by being cautious.

"Very. Dundas Hill has a glint in his eye, too, hasn't he?"

"You mean for me? How absurd."

"It's not absurd at all. He likes small women. Look at that museum he has."

"That's what Margaretta said." Alice gave a faint sigh. "Like you, she seems to think there is cause for jealousy. Only, of course, I know it isn't jealousy with you," she added calmly. "I wonder why Margaretta got so upset about those shoes. I wonder why she didn't tell us they were Camilla's—if she knew they were. I really think the child enjoys being mysterious. It's her father's fault for the kind of life he makes her live. She's just too sensitive."

"You know what happens when a woman starts to reform a man's household. Good luck to you, my pet. Dundas is a thoroughly worthy person. And if you really won't go back to England—"

"Felix, how dare you!" Alice burst out, aware that he always did this to her, always turned the tables on some grievance so that it was she in the wrong.

"Little Alice!" he said in his caressing voice.

Alice jerked away from him.

"Once I believed the things you said, heaven help me!"

"And it doesn't hurt too much to disbelieve them?"

"It doesn't hurt at all."

"Good. That's the place we wanted to get to. Believe me, Alice, it's only gifted people who get to that place."

He almost sounded as if he were trying to convince himself, as if his precious ego were hurt. (*Oh, Felix, try your blarney on Katherine Thorpe, or any other beautiful woman who comes along. In future I'm only going to fall in love with sensible sober men whom I can trust.)*

They had reached the gate of the cottage. Felix pushed it open and let her precede him to the door. It had begun to rain again in slow heavy drops. There was nothing but the dark sky and the darker trees.

"Take that coat off and put it away and don't wear it again!" Felix said. "Now you've had your curiosity satisfied—"

"Felix, Camilla was mercenary. She really was. The fact that someone gave her a fur coat wouldn't prevent her keeping it when she married another man."

"Never mind Camilla. We're tired of the subject of Camilla." His kiss as he took her in his arms was hard and brief. "That's just for good luck. Get yourself away from here. It's a pity you came, as things have turned out. For heaven's sake, can't you go back to England? Then I'll stop having a conscience about you."

He pushed her inside and pulled the door shut after her. Alice stood in the dark hall trembling. Then she collected herself enough to strike a match and fumble her way to the bedroom to light the candles.

The evening was over. Felix had kissed her again. But it had been a valedictory kiss. She was done with; Camilla was done with; there was a new star in the sky. It annoyed him that his old stars lingered. He developed a conscience about them.

Alice felt immeasurably forlorn. She slipped out of the squirrel coat and threw it on the bed. How unfair it was that Camilla had a surplus of lovers, while she mourned for the sadness of a single faithless one.

She was only glad that Felix had not stayed to see her weep.

It was after she had put the light out and was in bed that she heard a man's voice, talking softly somewhere outside.

"Come on," it was saying. "Come on, confound you. Say your piece. Tell me what you know, or I'll wring your blasted neck."

There was a muffled squawk, then a flapping of wings. The voice said, "Confound you!" again, and footsteps went down the path.

Alice sank down in bed with a half-hysterical giggle of relief. It had only been Felix talking to Webster. The silly boy, thinking a bird would wake up and talk at midnight.

It was in the morning that she discovered the diaries, which she had hidden under the mattress of her bed (a stupid obvious place, she now realized), were missing.

They would have been taken, of course, while she and Katherine had been lightheartedly dressing up Margaretta last night.

By one of the three D's, the one who was most afraid of what the diaries might contain.

VI

THE NEXT AFTERNOON when Dalton Thorpe called
for her in the long cream car Alice had a feeling of
being in another world. Not a very easy world. The
low car gliding along the wet tree-dark roads seemed
out of place in this rugged country, and the man
driving it, with his long somber face, his well-cut
clothes and polished manner, belonged no more than
his car did. Alice noticed his expensive calf shoes.
How should it happen that a farmer living in mountain country dressed like someone would meet in a
London club?

To Alice all her life acting had been second nature.
For diversion or convenience she was always escaping from herself and being someone else—one of her
mother's talkative friends, the gardener's boy with
his bashful stammer, the girl in school who most lent
herself to caricature, the clown in the theatrical
company. Since coming here she had found herself,
surrounded with Camilla's friends, perpetually being
Camilla, gay, casual, flirtatious. It was in a subcon-

scious effort to account for Camilla's actions. It seemed necessary to get inside Camilla's skin, especially where her men friends were concerned. Especially the one who had stolen the diaries.

Who am I this afternoon? she wondered. Camilla, thrilled to the soul at being driven by such a superior male, or Alice, not interested in superior males, but thinking wistfully of the comfort of Dundas' haphazard house and his affectionate regard for his "small ladies"? Did Felix's mocking voice come into her longing? *I had better be Camilla*, she decided.

She tried to talk to her driver, but he was a taciturn person for all his air of polish. Camilla, too, would have found him so at first, but nothing daunted Camilla. Therefore nothing should daunt her.

"Your sister is so beautiful, Mr. Thorpe. I just can't help thinking of her. And so kind, too, to invite me, a perfect stranger, to visit her."

"Katherine likes company," he answered shortly.

"She said she saw so few people. Do you live in a very isolated part, Mr. Thorpe?"

"Comparatively. When it rains the river rises. We get cut off occasionally."

Alice cast a glance at the rain misting on the windshield. The heavy clouds were down to the base of the mountains. There could have been no mountain there, only a flat plain saturated in rain and woolly cloud.

"Oh, I should think Katherine would hate that," she said as vivaciously as possible. "Does that happen often?"

"Four or five times a year, perhaps." Then Dalton Thorpe made a remark of his own. Without turning his handsome hawklike profile he asked, "How long are you staying here, Miss Ashton? It can't be very entertaining staying in that house alone."

"No—I admit I have a grudge against Camilla, going off like that. But she always was the most impulsive creature. Did you ever see anything of this mysterious stranger she apparently has had up her sleeve?"

His answer was completely uninformative. "I go out very little."

"Oh. Then no one has seen him. No, I don't imagine I shall stay very long in the cottage. I'll just wait and find out what has really happened to Camilla—for my own peace of mind more than anything."

He shot her a sideways look out of his long dark eyes.

"What do you mean? Don't you believe she is safely married?"

Alice gave a light laugh. "What a peculiar word to use, Mr. Thorpe. Safely. Do you know, that's just the word that occurs to me."

She thought his hands tightened on the wheel. She couldn't be sure. He had the same thin hard hands as his sister, and the knuckles were prominent all the time. But she did know that he was not at ease and that he disliked her being there. Her instinct told her that he was concealing something. She was almost sure he was the man who had slipped down to the cottage last night and taken the diaries. She was conscious of an inner trembling that was not so much fear as excitement. Something, she felt sure, was going to come out of this visit. But she was uncomfortably aware that whatever happened might not be very pleasant, or—again that word—safe.

It was only to be expected that the farmhouse would be as unexpected as the car and the Thorpes themselves. It was a white wooden house, completely modern, with large low windows built for the sun that seemed so rarely to shine. It was surrounded by smooth green lawns, with the bush cut back and controlled at a discreet distance. The farm outbuildings were also at a discreet distance, so that the white house stood alone, shining against the dark background like Katherine's beauty shone in a crowd.

"What a lovely house," Alice exclaimed, aware of the first excited impression the house must have made on Camilla, who loved the slightest hint of luxury.

"I built it," Dalton answered.

"Recently?"

"Three years ago." He drew the car up outside the dark-blue front door and, getting out, went around to open the car door for Alice.

"What made you come to this part of the world? I mean, it's magnificent, but if you haven't been born in it don't you find it a little gloomy sometimes?"

Dalton had his closed uncommunicative look. What a difficult person he was to get to know. How had Camilla discovered the key to his heart? She must have done so, for there was that note, *Have missed you so much, darling.* Dalton Thorpe looked too self-contained ever to miss anyone, but probably his nature, beneath that reserve, was extremely passionate.

"We like it," he answered briefly.

At that moment the front door opened and there was Katherine running down the steps excitedly, crying, "Alice darling, how nice to see you. I've looked forward to this so much."

She put her arms around Alice in an affectionate embrace. Her ardent welcome was as surprising as her brother's reserve. Then she went ahead up the steps, saying, "Come in out of this horrid rain. Sometimes I think I will go mad if it keeps on raining. But when the sun shines the mountains seem to press down on me, so really I don't know which is the worst."

Alice followed her through a wide ivory-paneled hall into a large comfortable room in which a log fire burnt. She noticed that Dalton Thorpe had not followed them, so she could say, "But your brother says you like it here."

Katherine turned. Her black eyes were bright with some sharply felt emotion.

"Oh, *he* says so. Yes, indeed, he says so. Didn't we have fun with Margaretta last night? But the silly little creature spoilt it all at the end."

"It was because of the shoes," said Alice deliberately. "They were Camilla's, you know."

Katherine looked at her blankly. "Were they? Oh, I didn't know that. Well, what of it? Did she think she would catch a plague from them? And I *was* enjoying dressing her up." (Odd, the ownership of the shoes seemed to mean nothing to her. She had a mind like a fantail, flittering here and there, never settling on one thing.)

"Now we will have tea right away and then we will

talk," she went on. "I want to know all about you. Everything. Perhaps I seem inquisitive, but I see so *few* people. Dalton makes hermits of us."

Tea was brought in by an elderly woman in a black dress. She had exceptionally large strong hands, Alice noticed, and a hard face. Alice began to be sorry for Katherine, who was so lovely and yet who had to live a lonely life with a taciturn brother and this hard-faced woman. She noticed that Katherine said, "Thank you, Mrs. Jobbett," in an almost nervous voice, and that she didn't recover her animation until the woman was out of the room. Then she began to chatter again, her lovely face full of mobility.

"How long will you stay over here? Do stay a long time so we can see a lot of each other. What do you do for a living? Couldn't you get a job here? Couldn't you teach in the school?"

Alice laughed. "I'm not a schoolteacher. Besides, Camilla may be coming back even though she is married. She hasn't actually resigned. You'd like that, wouldn't you?"

"Oh, Camilla. No, she wasn't trustworthy." Everything she had seemed to feel yesterday was dismissed. "No, I wouldn't like her back. Neither would Dalton. No, we'd rather have you." She gave Alice her brilliant smile. "Do stay, won't you?"

It was then that Alice had her first feeling of uneasiness. It was something to do with Katherine's hands, the way the knuckles seemed too large for the skin that covered them. When she was old they would be claws. And it definitely wasn't true that Dalton would rather have her than Camilla, because there was the evidence of that note that Tottie had delivered. But, of course, Dalton wouldn't tell a sister who chattered as Katherine did all his secrets.

A few moments later Dalton came in for tea. He watched his sister pouring it. Indeed, he seemed to be watching her all the time. He maintained his usual reserve, but his long dark eyes missed nothing.

The rain outside had become harder, and, listening to it on the window, Katherine said vivaciously, "Oh, good, Alice. If it keeps on raining like that you'll have to stay all night. We should love that. Shouldn't we, Dalton?"

"It would require exceptionally hard rain to flood the river within a few hours," her brother answered.

"Well, never mind the flooded river. Alice can stay in any case. Can't you, darling?"

The poor girl was lonely. She said so often enough. One had to be sorry for her. But the thought of spending a night here filled Alice with a queer apprehension.

"I should like to get back, if possible. One can't have two women disappearing from the schoolhouse without explanation."

"But who would worry about you? Aren't you alone?"

"Well—Dundas." Again Alice was thinking of Dundas with affection and security.

"That odd little man," said Katherine. "He has eyes like a tiger."

"A tiger?" said Dalton suddenly. "How absurd."

"Well, one of those cats. Not just a tame pussy."

"Really, Kay, your imagination behaves in the strangest way."

Katherine flushed and drooped. Alice got the impression that she was a little afraid of her brother just as she was of the housekeeper. Goodnaturedly she came to the girl's rescue.

"Sometimes Dundas' eyes are like a cat's at night. But he is the kindest person. And then there's Felix—I mean Mr. Dodsworth." (Would Felix worry about her and try to find out where she was? If she disappeared she thought he would, if only out of curiosity.)

"Oh yes, Felix," Katherine cried vivaciously. "He's sweet. Do you know him well, Alice?"

"Well enough."

"But how interesting. Dalton, I think we should ask Felix to dinner one night."

The repressive scowl on her brother's forehead deepened.

"Isn't he driving the bus?"

"But that's what makes him so interesting. He's so versatile. I thought he was extraordinarily nice."

Her face was glowing with enthusiasm. If Felix were there now he would know he had made one of his easiest conquests to date. And it would no doubt go to his charming faithless head. At the same time Alice had the impression that if Dalton could prevent it Katherine would not see Felix again. He was a snob. A broken-down actor-cum-bus driver would get no encouragement from him. It was unreasonable of her to feel that small measure of relief about someone who had deliberately walked out of her life.

Katherine had sensed her brother's mood. She was downcast for a few moments, then she made a determined effort to regain her spirits.

"Anyway," she said brightly, "the immediate

thing is that if it rains too hard we keep Alice all night. And then we really can have a long, long talk.''

It was strange how, after her distress the other day, and her agitation last night during the episode of the fur coat, she seemed to have put Camilla completely out of her mind.

VII

KATHERINE'S BEDROOM upstairs had the luxury that
one had come to expect in this house. The white
quilted satin bed covering, the pastel-pink carpet and
the white ruffled curtains looped with rose-colored
velvet were a perfect setting for her dark beauty.
Alice said so enthusiastically, and Katherine sighed
and said, "Every time we move I change my color
scheme. That's the only way it's fun moving. I suppose you think it's silly having a room like this way up
in the mountains. In a way it is, but Dalton thinks we
may stay here a little longer than most places, and,
anyway, I like things. I lie in bed and pretend I'm still
in Honolulu or on the Cote d'Azur."

"Have you moved a lot?" Alice asked unnecessar-
ily.

"A lot?" For a moment Katherine looked blank,
almost as if she couldn't remember. It was the dazed
look of the constant traveler who wakes and can't
remember where he is. "Oh yes. I can't remember us
being more than a year in any place, except here, and

now it's nearly three years. And if we stay much longer I shall go mad." She pressed her thin sharp fingers into her temples, leaving red marks on the white skin. She had a distracted look, as if the place were indeed affecting her mind. "But Dalton likes it. He said when we came that this was the kind of place he'd been looking for for years. So he built the house and bought a lot of cows and things, and here we've stayed. To rot."

"Oh, surely not. There's the hotel so close."

"Yes, but people never stay there long enough for one to make friends even if Dalton let me meet them. He doesn't, you know. He prefers me to be alone. He didn't even want you to come tonight."

Alice was startled, although she had already sensed that fact.

"But that, surely, is because I remind him of Camilla. I think—didn't you say he was fond of her?"

"Oh, Camilla?" It almost seemed as if Camilla, like the other places in which she had lived, was slipping out of Katherine's mind. Or had her brother warned her that the Camilla theme was unpopular? "Do you know, I think you have a much nicer face than Camilla. Now we know she wasn't trustworthy we don't care nearly so much about her going. She used us, you know. She took our hospitality and—" Her hesitation was curiously significant. "—other things, and then just went off without a word of thanks."

"But it was strange about her leaving the fur coat."

"Oh, that," said Katherine absently. "But it was only squirrel."

The thing was too puzzling. Last night Katherine had seemed almost to faint at the sight of the coat. Now she dismissed it lightly as a thing of no account. After all, she, who had moved at a whim all over the world, might turn up her nose at a squirrel coat, but Camilla Mason never would. That was the angle from which to look at it. It really seemed that Katherine and not Camilla was the one who was faithless to a friendship.

Already she had changed the subject and was saying, with her black eyes sparkling, "Let's dress for dinner tonight, shall we? It would be such fun."

"But I'm afraid I'm not staying to dinner. And, besides, I haven't brought any change of clothes."

"Oh, but you are staying, of course. Listen to that rain. I can lend you a dress. Come and choose one."

She flung open her wardrobe and disclosed a bewildering array of clothes, suits, dresses, evening gowns.

"If that poor kid Margaretta had been here last night we'd have had no trouble in dressing her. But I believe she likes being shabby." She lifted out a black chiffon. "I got this in Paris. It's three years old, but black doesn't date so much. Or here's the green thing I got in Rio. I never wore it. This is one I had sent from New York. I took the rhinestones off— they glittered too much."

"But where do you wear all these?" Alice asked in bewilderment.

"Nowhere." Her beautiful black eyes surveyed

Alice. "You think I'm mad, don't you? But one must do something. Even a hermit must do something."

Alice said uneasily, "They're all beautiful, but really I must go home. It's getting dark now. Will your brother mind taking me?"

"You can't go. Listen to the rain and the wind."

"It isn't raining very hard now." This was true, although it was also true that the wind was rising, and the night promised to be wild and stormy.

"But it's much too cold and unpleasant to go out. I had your room readied in case I could persuade you to stay." Katherine smiled her brilliant wistful smile. "Do," she begged.

"Why, another time I'd like to. But tonight—" Alice couldn't have explained her uneasiness. It was somehow wrapped up in the luxury of this lonely house, in the ridiculous surplus of clothes that hung in the wardrobe, in the careless way Katherine had dismissed Camilla as if she were scarcely even a memory, in the fact that Dalton had never wanted her to come and that as far as he was concerned she was quite unwelcome. And lastly, quite unreasonably, in that silly remark Katherine had made about Dundas' eyes being like a tiger's. No smile could have been less apt.

Katherine was pouting, her face that of a spoiled child.

"How unkind you are, Alice. Very well, we'll go down and find Dalton. You shall just have a drink with him before you go."

Dalton was in the lounge downstairs, and even his façade of good manners couldn't conceal the fact that he was relieved Alice had her coat on.

"Alice is just going to have a drink before she goes," Katherine said in her vivacious manner. "I can't persuade her to stay. You get her one, will you, Dalton dear, while I tell Mrs. Jobbett we're not having a guest for dinner after all."

As she went out Alice heard the wind buffeting against the house. It seemed to have got very dark. Although they were invisible behind the deep mist, suddenly she was peculiarly conscious of the mountains looming close, as if to shut them in this world of wind and rain.

"What will you drink, Miss Ashton?" Dalton asked in his courteous voice. "Will you have a brandy? It's a cold night to go out."

"Thank you," said Alice. "I'm sorry to take you out, too, on a night like this."

"Not at all. I'm used to it." Now that she was going, his manner was subtly more friendly. "Do you know, I've never been a farmer before, but I find it extraordinarily fascinating. And there's something about this kind of country that appeals to me. I should like to be able to stay here a long time."

"Is there any reason why you wouldn't be able to stay?" Alice asked lightly. The question was asked at random, but to her disappointment it had the effect of closing Dalton in his reserve again.

"My sister has got into the habit of moving about, as she has probably told you. She may find it too quiet here."

"She told me she gets very lonely," Alice said.

"Yes." His fingers were gripping the stem of his glass. The prominent Thorpe knuckles shone in the light. Alice thought she heard him add under his breath, "It is necessary," but at that moment Katherine came hurrying in, crying, "A drink for me, Dalton. It's so cold."

But she didn't look cold. Her cheeks were glowing. Her eyes sparkled like jewels. She looked enchantingly lovely.

Dalton poured her a drink, then put his own glass down and said, "Excuse me, Miss Ashton. I'll go and bring the car around. I think we ought to get on our way before the storm gets worse."

As he went out Katherine suddenly giggled.

"He's so serious, poor old Dalton," she explained. "If he wouldn't be so serious!" She sighed. Alice noticed all at once that her hair shone with raindrops. There was mud on her shoes.

"You've been out in the rain," she said.

"Yes, I had to. Mrs. Jobbett was down at the cottage. Our servants live down there. Mrs. Jobbett and Tottie. This house isn't really big enough to accommodate servants. Besides, Dalton and I like having it to ourselves at night. Mrs. Jobbett goes home after dinner."

A flurry of rain swept across the darkening windows. Suddenly the front door banged and Dalton came marching into the room, his thin dark brows drawn terrifyingly together.

"The car's punctured. I'm sorry, Miss Ashton, I can't take you home. If it were just one tire it could be changed, but it's two. I haven't two spares."

The tips of his nostrils were white, his cheekbones stuck out as prominently as his knuckles. His eyes were fixed on Katherine, and she, unexpectedly, gave her little giggle again. That, somehow, was the most disturbing of all. Alice knew the reason now for the muddy shoes and the wet hair. Her sense of disquiet deepened into something that was almost fear.

"Why, now Alice will have to stay," Katherine said delightedly, completely ignoring her brother's anger. "What a good thing I had a room prepared for you, darling. Isn't this fun!"

So all the day Katherine had known that somehow she would be persuaded to stay. But why this desire to have her stay?

To Alice's surprise Dalton said nothing more at all. As abruptly as he had come in he went out of the room. And Alice was thinking, *One night Camilla didn't come home either. Felix and Dundas and I sat in the cottage and discussed what could have kept her. We thought it might have been a flooded river. We didn't think of punctured tires. And she never came back. . . .*

"Don't look so glum, darling," she heard Katherine saying in her light lively voice. "Mrs. Jobbett's a very good cook. We'll give you a good dinner. And your room's rather a pet. Come and I'll show it to you."

Alice, with all the considerable stubbornness of which her small body was capable, refused the offer of one of Katherine's dinner dresses and went down to dinner in the plain gray wool jersey in which she had come. She fully expected Katherine, who apparently loved dramatic situations, to burst in in white brocade or black chiffon, but after all Katherine's good manners were stronger than her love of the dramatic, and she did no more than tuck a white camellia in her black hair.

Dinner, served by the harsh-faced Mrs. Jobbett with her curiously masculine hands, was a rather silent meal. Alice was ashamed of herself for sulking a little, but the whole thing was so absurdly childish. Punctured tires indeed! And it was better to sulk than to give way to that cool unease that lay like a shadow over her mind. (Why had they planned to keep her here?)

Katherine chatted valiantly about places where the sun had always shone. But she was aware of her brother's displeasure and her voice had an undertone of defiance. And all the time the storm was increasing, the trees cracking and roaring in the wind, and the rain beating in sudden squalls against the windows. Alice found herself constantly thinking that there might be lambs out in the storm. A silly little white lamb, Felix had called her. A wretched rash intruding fool. . . .

But how Felix would admire Katherine with the white flower shining in smooth dark hair.

"Alice, you don't talk nearly as much as Camilla did," Katherine said at last fretfully. Then, "Poor Camilla."

"Why poor?" Alice queried. Suddenly her heartbeats seemed louder than the sound of her voice. Camilla had gone out one day and had never come back. . . .

Dalton said in his crisp disapproving voice, "This coffee's cold. Can't we ever teach that woman to serve hot coffee?"

"Well, darling, you know I don't like Mrs. Jobbett. You know I'd like her to go."

But this suggestion Dalton did not approve of, either.

"Apart from the coffee she's perfectly satisfactory."

"Camilla used to say 'How can you live with that woman?' Do you think that, too, Alice?" Katherine asked plaintively.

"Never mind Camilla. We won't talk of Camilla."

"Oh, Dalton darling!" Katherine came around the table to lay her narrow hands on either side of his face. "You're in a mood. Now you see, Alice, why I long for other people. Dalton gets moody and I have no one to talk to."

Alice was abruptly sorry for her. Then she remembered the punctured tires and she refused to be drawn out of her sulkiness. The odd uneasy evening drew on until at last she could, with good manners, excuse herself and go upstairs to the charmingly furnished room that was hers for the night.

There was someone in the room. With relief Alice recognized the round freckled face of Tottie, who was turning down the bed.

"Hello, Tottie," she said. "I'm sorry you have an extra bed to make."

Tottie grinned, her friendly face beautifully ordinary and comforting.

"That's all right, miss. I'm used to it. I did it for Miss Mason often enough."

"Did she used to—expect to stay?" Alice asked cautiously.

"Well, not at first, perhaps. Miss Thorpe used to find some excuse, I think. She's crazy for company. But after, she used to stay whenever she wanted to.

You can guess why that was." Tottie winked broadly. "Him. I've put a hot bottle in. It's turned that cold tonight."

"Thank you, Tottie." Alice was almost gay in her relief. So even if Camilla had been tricked, as she had been, to stay here at first, later she had come of her own free will. There was nothing queer about it after all. She could sleep soundly and go home in the morning and explain to Dundas, who would be worried off his kind little head, where she had been.

Tottie flicked some dust off the dressing-table and turned to go out.

"But if I was you," she whispered suddenly, her face stuck around the door, "I'd turn the key in the lock tonight. Just in case."

Alice flew to the door.

"Why, Tottie? Why?"

But Tottie was already halfway downstairs, and the sight of Dalton Thorpe lighting a leisurely pipe down in the hall was making her hurry more than ever. Alice could not call her back.

Lock the door? It seemed so discourteous, so absurd, in this pleasant house. Supposing Katherine came to talk and found her guest had locked herself in? No, it was an impossible thing to do. But *why* had Tottie suggested it?

It took a great deal of will power not to follow Tottie's suggestion. Likewise, Alice had to force herself to undress and put on the pale-blue satin nightdress that Katherine had had spread out on the bed for her. She shivered as the cool material touched her skin. She got into bed and put out the light, and then lay rigid in the darkness, listening to the wind beating against the house. Where was Camilla? In the littl carnation-scented house Camilla's absence ha seemed a naughty prank; her sketchy diary anc Webster's significant remarks had the touch of a comic opera crime. Now, her imagination distorted by her surroundings, the mystery of Camilla was assuming a sinister quality that surely it did not possess. Dalton did not like Camilla's name mentioned. Camilla had deliberately come here to see him. Tottie had said it was wise to lock the bedroom door. Perhaps Camilla used to lock it. Perhaps one night she had forgotten. . . .

Katherine's light voice at the door made her start up.

"Are you asleep, darling? Oh, I'm sorry I disturbed you. I just wanted to know if you were comfortable."

Alice switched on the light and saw Katherine in a turquoise-colored velvet dressing-gown, her hair brushed down on her shoulders. She looked so beautiful and so kind that Alice was ashamed of her nervousness.

"Yes, I'm quite comfortable, thank you."

Katherine came forward.

"Alice, that Felix Dodsworth I met last night— what kind of a man is he? You've known him for a long time, haven't you?"

"For a year or so," Alice answered guardedly. "He's all right."

"What a mediocre answer, darling. I thought he was perfectly sweet." She began to smile, a slow secretive smile. One thin finger rubbed up and down her cheek. "And I rather think he likes me a little. Or perhaps more than a little. He's just telephoned now."

"Oh?" Alice couldn't keep the startled interest out of her voice. Had Felix discovered her absence? Was he worrying about her?

"He wants to see me again. As soon as possible, he said. He sounded—" Again came the satisfied secret smile. "Well, you know how impetuous a man can sound. But I know Dalton won't approve. Dalton's *quite* a snob." She sighed. "But I mustn't keep you awake with my small affairs. Good night, Alice. Sleep well. It's so wonderful having you."

D is so impetuous, Alice was thinking. *Strange, that was the word Camilla used, too.* Felix was a stupid fool, getting tangled up with women like this. Couldn't he pay less attention to females and more to his career? At this rate he would be driving the bus from Hokitika to the glaciers for the rest of his life.

So it hadn't been her absence he was worried about after all. For the second time Alice lay down and put out the light. She had an inclination to cry. She felt so, alone, so unwanted. She would never write in a diary *D won't wait*. She imagined she could see Katherine's lovely face floating in the darkness, and behind it Felix's—narrow, mischievous, alive with interest.

But at least Felix had done one thing for her. He had taken her mind off the unlocked door and the intangible danger that might lurk in this house.

She slept and dreamed about Camilla. Camilla was laughing and whispering, "You'd better lock the door. It's wisest." What a queer laugh Camilla had developed: throaty and malicious. She was actually turning the key in the lock and laughing in that deep gurgle.

It was so peculiar that it wakened Alice out of her sleep. She opened her eyes wide, trying to throw off the nightmare. The wind was buffeting against the house, and even the square of her window was scarcely less dark than the rest of the room. Something was moving in the darkness. It was the curtains swaying in and out, the rings on which they hung clinking faintly. The rain seemed to have stopped. Alice strained her eyes, trying to catch a reassuring glimpse of some stars. And at that moment there was a movement near the door and a voice whispered, "Camilla's here. Isn't that a joke?" Then there was that awful throaty laugh that hadn't been in her dream after all, but that existed in reality, and the door closed with a small bang.

Alice started up. She was jerked back as if she had received a blow. For a moment her mind refused to work. She lay petrified, her heart pounding until the bed shook. Someone stood behind her at the head of the bed in the darkness. Who was it? What were they doing? She moved her lips to speak, but no sound came.

The wind hit the house in a long swoop and the curtains gave their innocent clinking.

Like ice in a glass on a hot day, she thought. The icy perspiration had started out on her brow. There was no movement behind her. The room, apart from the slight sway of the curtains, was utterly still.

No one could stand that still. One would hear

breathing. Alice licked her lips, and with a further effort contrived to produce a shaky voice: "Who's there?"

There was no answer. *Was* there someone there? If she could summon up enough courage to switch on the light she would know the truth.

She moved her head carefully, and again there was that queer tug, slighter now, not enough to restrain her from pressing the switch.

Light flooded the room. Alice turned her head sharply, and the pain of her pulled hair showed her what had happened. There was no one behind her at the head of the bed, but someone had crept in and tied the frivolous blue ribbon that was around her hair to the bedpost.

It was a silly trick, a completely childish trick. But for some reason Alice, with a shaking hand, unloosing the ribbon, was filled with horror. Free, she sprang out of bed and stood on the soft lamb's-wool rug trembling. Then she began frantically to pull off Katherine's nightdress and get into her clothes. She knew that she could not spend the rest of the night in this house. She couldn't spend another five minutes here. She had to get away at once and find Dundas, Felix, tell them what was going on, tell them that she suspected Camilla was being kept, for some utterly unknown reason, by the Thorpes.

Tottie had said, "Lock your door." Tottie knew something. But one couldn't stop to find and question Tottie now. One had to get away quickly.

Her fingers trembled so that she could scarcely pull on her shoes. The wind was like massive hands against the house, pushing it and shaking it. But the noise of it would cover any sound she might make going down the stairs. She dared not put on lights lest her flight be discovered. Her mind shied away from conjectures as to what might happen if she were discovered. The whole thing was a gigantic nightmare. Camilla's little cottage with its leaking roof and draughty windows was the haven to which she must escape.

Once, halfway down the dark stairs, she thought she heard that malicious chuckling again. For one moment she froze. Then, disregarding caution, she stumbled down the remainder of the stairs, groped her way down the long hall and found the key in the front door.

As she opened the door the wind swarmed in. Like cold water in her face, it restored her to sanity. She hesitated on the doorstep, thinking of the long walk down the wet windy roads. But to go back to that pretty bedroom was worse. The elements were infinitely preferable to unknown dangers.

Somewhere in the house a clock struck one. Suddenly the wind seized the door and banged it behind her. With a little gasp of fright and relief Alice knew that now she couldn't go back. She must go to the safety of the cottage.

VIII

A PALE MOON was struggling through the clouds when Alice at last saw the dark bulk of the hotel and the dim road winding down to the cottage. She sighed with weary relief, and continued her trudge through the stormy night. Now that she was within reach of the cottage she was almost inclined to chuckle at her comic plight. She had a blister on each heel, was wet through, and buffeted to the point of exhaustion. She had stumbled along six miles of dark stony roads just because someone had played a practical joke on her. Where was her sense of humor? she wondered.

But humor did not really come into this situation. Instinct told her that the whole thing had been deadly serious. It had something to do with Camilla. She could not forget that whispered voice: "Camilla's here." Was Camilla really there? She had to tell Dundas and Felix as quickly as possible and have the thing investigated.

The sky was clearing in patches, and a shoulder of one of the mountains, broad and glistening white, shone against the sky. The wind off the snow was so cold that Alice, for all her exercise, was shivering constantly.

If there had been a light showing in Dundas' house she would have gone in there and told her story. But the old house among the trees was dark and silent. Alice thought of Dundas sleeping warm and undisturbed, and had a sudden longing for his kind serious voice. Felix in all likelihood would burst into loud guffaws and say, "Little Alice, can't you take a joke?" but Dundas, she knew, would be sympathetic and comforting. He would not think she had behaved like a little frightened fool in running away from the Thorpe house at midnight.

She trudged around the bend of the road and saw the dark trees surrounding the cottage. In ten minutes she would be able to creep into bed herself and sleep until her exhaustion was gone and the things distorted in her tired mind had resumed a normal shape. It must be almost daylight, but there was no light except that of the fleeting moonlight. Wait! Was that a light through the trees in the direction of the cottage? Was there a light in the window?

Alice stood still to look. The wind shook the trees violently back and forth, and as they moved there was the glimpse of a faint yellow light, no more than starlight. Or candlelight. She began to run, stumbling on the uneven road. When she came in sight of the cottage the windows were dark. Of course there had been no light, she told herself in relief. It had been reflected moonlight. All was quiet and undisturbed. In a few minutes she could sleep.

She pushed the gate open, leaning against it because the path down from the cottage was like a funnel through which the wind swept in a great force. The tall ngaio tree at the side of the house bent and cracked. The thinning clouds moved over the moon and parted, and pale light shone down on the doorstep, light just strong enough to show Alice the dark object that lay there.

She bent over it curiously. Then she gave a cry of dismay and went down on her knees to pick up the limp body of Webster, the magpie. His head hung down; his long sharp beak was slightly open. His neck was twisted; he was quite dead.

Wet through and shivering violently, Alice crouched with the bird in her hands, trying to think. Someone had killed Webster because he talked. It was her fault, really. She had chattered about the uncanniness of Webster's language; she had let people think that his unconscious imitation of words and sentences was giving away secrets. About Camilla and some unknown man. Not an unknown man. One of the three D's. They had all heard her chatter about Webster. "He's like someone's conscience," she had said. Which man had thought Webster was his conscience?

Then, like a miniature record playing over and over, she was suddenly remembering Felix's voice last night, "Confound you! Tell me what you know or I'll wring your neck!"

The moon was hidden again, the light gone. Alice could scarcely see the bird in her hands. She got slowly to her feet, her legs so weak that she could scarcely stand. She put out her hand to open the door. It was open behind her. She was sure of that, for she turned sharply and almost fell forward into the darkness. Then suddenly, as if obeying a signal, the ngaio tree cracked sharply and there was a frantic beating of leaves, like a wave breaking. That sound was the last thing of which Alice was aware.

IX

HER HEAD WAS aching badly and there was a weight on top of it. At first Alice could not exert herself to open her eyes. She moved cautiously, and felt the separate ache in each limb. "I've caught a chill," she thought vaguely.

She opened her eyes slowly, narrowing them against the hurting light, and saw a row of white bobbles on a white counterpane. Puzzled, her eyes strayed farther on a white wallpaper with a faded pink stripe like candy, an old-fashioned dressing-table with long mirror and innumerable drawers, a massive wardrobe. She still could not absorb the information her eyes gave her. She lay staring at the wallpaper for a long time, and it got mixed in her mind with a dress she had once had, a cotton dress that she had worn on a picnic, and she had got it stained with blackberry juice. She began to search for the stain on the wallpaper, and suddenly, as her eyes moved, she saw someone staring at her.

At first she could not identify the face. The heavy

features were familiar, and yet they had no connection with the wallpaper and the candy-striped frock belonging to her childhood.

She opened her mouth to speak. The face came nearer. It swam before her blurred vision, and for a reason she knew she should be able to remember but which eluded her she was suddenly shrinking into the pillows, filled with terror.

"You're awake, are you?" came a prosaic voice. "I'd better tell Daddy."

The face cleared, and at last Alice recognized Margaretta's scowling brows and broad cheekbones.

Her limbs went slack with relief. It was only Margaretta. She was no one of whom to be frightened.

"Wait!" she said. She had thought her voice would be strong, but it came out in a kind of croaking whisper. "Tell me, what am I doing here?" The candy-striped wallpaper. . . .It was peculiarly soothing, like a return to her childhood.

"You're ill," Margaretta told her bluntly. "You've got slight concussion, and a chill, the doctor said. You've been talking a bit silly, I must say."

"Concussion?" said Alice perplexedly. So that was why her head ached so badly, why her mind was so muddled. (But what was it that she was frightened about?)

"A tree fell on you in the storm," said Margaretta dispassionately. "It's lucky you weren't killed. Daddy found you and brought you here. We've been wondering what you were doing out in the storm, but you can tell us when you're better." She moved towards the door. "I'll tell Daddy you're awake."

What was that dark shadow over her mind? Alice closed her eyes, trying to think. The darkness came down like a blessing. She must have gone sound asleep, for when she opened her eyes again, to her astonishment the whole room was dark save for a silver ribbon of moonlight across the floor.

Her head felt better and clearer, although her body still ached. She lay quietly, not seeking memory but letting things drift idly into her mind. The candy-striped dress had been in her childhood. Since then she had traveled, she had been to school in New Zealand, and, the war over at last, had spent two unhappy summers with her mother dragging around the smart hotels in the South of France and on the Italian lakes. After that she had made her decision: she had left home and contrived to get jobs connected with the theater. For a while she had been a very inefficient secretary to a theatrical manager, then, nearer to the stage, she had been a dresser. Soon after that Felix had discovered her being Ophelia as she tidied the dressing-room and pressed costumes. Apparently he had listened for quite a long time. She had been overcome with embarrassment—she would never forget looking up and seeing him with his head cocked on one side, his eyes narrowed with interest, his dark hair ruffled—but it had resulted in her being invited to join his company, whose keenness and optimism compensated for its lack of money, and to set out on its world tour.

Alice frowned as the fragments drifted into her memory. How had that small one-class rather drab ship that had sailed from Tilbury brought her to this bed in a room with pink-striped wallpaper, and a wardrobe large enough to conceal a body?

A body? Unease stirred in her. What had produced that grim thought? Now her headache was coming back, and she was trying to think. Just beyond the shadow in her mind was knowledge which she didn't care to remember. There were birds in it, black heavy birds that weighed down her hands, and rain and wind. And somewhere Felix's black eyes laughing.

Trying to escape from thought, Alice was abruptly aware of a sound. It came from over her head, and it seemed like slow footsteps going backwards and forwards, muffled footsteps, slightly dragging, as if whoever was walking about did not want to arouse the house.

And suddenly there was one idea of trememdous magnitude in her mind. The door. Was it locked?

Without knowing the reason for her urgency Alice got out of bed and staggered across the floor. The shaft of moonlight swung up and down dizzily. She had to clutch the end of the bed, and then a corner of the massive wardrobe. Somehow she reached the door and turned the handle.

The door failed to open. It was locked.

Curiously, the shock of this discovery brought her back to reality. She remembered everything now. Standing shivering, her heavy head leaned against the door, she knew that she was in Dundas' house, for Margaretta had been with her that afternoon. And there was no necessity for a door to be locked in Dundas' house. It was in the Thorpe house that Tottie had said, "Lock your door," and it was there that someone had played that terrifying practical joke on her.

Why was the door locked in Dundas' house? Who had taken the precaution of locking in someone who was apparently helpless in bed?

In her normal health Alice was sure that she would not have got panicky. But now everything had the proportions of a nightmare. It was intolerable to be locked in a room. She couldn't stand it. She would go mad.

Frenziedly she began rattling the door handle and calling out. In the midst of her frenzy blackness swept over her in hot waves. She was scarcely aware of the door being opened, and only a little more conscious of tumbling into Dundas' arms.

"Alice," he was saying in a deeply concerned voice. "What is it, my dear? Did something frighten you? I thought you were sleeping. Margaretta said you had gone into a sound sleep and wouldn't likely wake till morning."

Alice clutched him weakly. She could feel that he had a thick wool dressing-gown on. The soft warmth of it was wonderfully comforting. She was so tired and weak that she never wanted to move away from it.

"Why was the door locked?" she asked, and began to repeat senselessly, "Why was it? Why was it?"

Dundas suddenly picked her up in his arms and carried her over to the bed. His eyes looking down at her had their night-enlarged pupils—it was curious how they made him look a different person at night—but his mouth was kind and gentle.

"Poor little girl! I'm sorry you got a fright about that. But Margaretta and I thought it was wise, just in case you woke up, you know. We couldn't risk you getting another chill by running out of the house."

"Oh," said Alice slowly. Now she was beginning to understand. "It was because I left the Thorpes' in the middle of the night."

"Never mind about that now." Dundas was gentle and reassuring. "We'll talk about that again. Now I'm going to make you a hot drink and you're to go back to sleep."

He went to move away, but Alice clutched at his arm.

"How long have I been here?"

"This is Tuesday night. Or rather Wednesday morning."

"That's two days nearly. But that's terrible!"

Dundas smiled. "Is it? I haven't thought so, except that your illness worried us a good deal."

"But what happened to Camilla in the meantime?" she cried.

He stiffened, almost imperceptibly.

"Camilla?"

"Yes—she's at the Thorpes'. They're hiding her there, for some reason. We've got to investigate. That's why I left there in the middle of the night."

Dundas said in his slow gentle way, "Don't you think you might be imagining that? You've had a bad knock. A branch of that ngaio tree caught the side of your head. It's lucky you weren't killed."

Alice's brain was swimming, but she stuck stubbornly to her story.

"The tree hadn't hit me then. I tell you, someone came in my room and whispered, 'Camilla's here.' It might have been Camilla herself. Though I can't imagine Camilla doing that horrid thing."

"What horrid thing?"

Somehow Alice didn't want to talk about her tied hair. It sounded so silly and childish, no one else would think it sinister. Even Dundas, in his sympathy, would only humor her.

"Never mind that. That was only incidental. But I know there's something queer going on at the Thorpes' and it has to be investigated. It's something to do with Camilla. Dalton Thorpe was crazy about her, you know. He's done something to her." Alice's voice was rising hysterically. "Don't look at me like that. It's true. Besides, there's Webster. Someone came that night and killed Webster. They were frightened of what he used to say. Someone with a guilty conscience. Dundas, we've got to investigate—"

His hand stroked her hair softly, reassuringly.

"Of course. Of course we'll investigate. I found the magpie, too. But I really think he was killed in a fight. He was badly pecked about the head."

"His neck was wrung," Alice persisted. She remembered so distinctly the wobbling head that no longer had any connection with Webster's pert precociousness. It was part of her nightmare, that dangling inert head.

"Perhaps," Dundas agreed soothingly. "But we won't talk of it now. It's two o'clock in the morning and nothing can be done until daylight. So I'm going

to bring you this drink and you're going to sleep.
You'll be surprised how things come back to normal
by daylight.''

Alice made one last effort.

"There's someone in this house, too, walking
about. You'll have to look."

Dundas laughed.

"Well, that was me. That's the easiest explanation
of all. I'm a very poor sleeper. I often walk about at
night, as Margaretta will tell you. I'm so sorry I
frightened you."

By the time Dundas came back with two glasses of
hot milk on a tray Alice had grown calmer. Dundas'
very sanity reduced her panic. He did not believe
Camilla was at the Thorpes', but even if she were
there she would be perfectly all right. That was what
his quiet confident manner told her. After all, it was
true that nothing could be accomplished at two
o'clock in the morning. And nothing at all could be
accomplished while one remained ill. It was her duty
to get well as quickly as possible so that she would be
able to go back to that tall elegant house of the
Thorpes and find out what really went on inside it.

She realized now that she shouldn't have run
away. Felix would despise her for it. Did Felix know
what had happened?

Dundas helped her up on her pillows. He wrapped
a woolly bed-jacket around her shoulders, fussing
like a woman.

"There you are, nice and cozy," he said in the
voice that was like thick black velvet, warm and soft
and comforting. "Drink this up and stop thinking.

Plenty of time to think when your head is functioning again. Eh?"

"You're very good to me," Alice murmured weakly.

"Not at all. Glad to be. It was heaven-sent that I found you."

Alice sank into the comfort of his voice and his care. It was with a sense of disloyalty that she asked the question at the surface of her mind.

"Does Felix know about this? Felix Dodsworth?"

"The bus driver? Yes, indeed." Dundas laughed, not altogether with appreciation. "He came in here like an avalanche. I'm afraid he thinks women make a habit of disappearing from the schoolhouse. He was relieved to find you were all right. Or comparatively all right. You talked a good deal of nonsense."

"What did I say?" Alice asked guardedly.

"Mostly what you've been saying to me now about this idea that Camilla is a prisoner at the Thorpes'."

"Oh," said Alice, glad that that was the only nonsense she had talked. She sipped her milk, and wondered if Felix had really been upset. Of course, he would be sad if anything had happened to her, but would he suffer an agony that could not be comforted?

It was almost absurd, the thought that Felix could be comfortless. There would always be some woman to stroke his brow . . .

"That's better," said Dundas in a pleased tone. "You're smiling."

"Am I?" Had she really smiled about a thing like that? Then perhaps she, too, was the kind who could be easily comforted. She looked at Dundas' round beaming face, and suddenly she wanted to draw her hand softly down his cheek. He was so kind.

She drank her milk and the nightmare receded more and more. Her head ached less and all at once her eyelids drooped.

"You're very sweet," said Dundas softly, "but you must go away."

Who else had said that she must go away? With an effort Alice opened her eyes wide.

"Why?"

"Because it's not right for you to stay here alone. Tomorrow or, if you're not well enough by then, the next day I'll drive you into Hokitika and you must catch the train home. I'm sure your brothers wouldn't like to know you were staying here alone and having accidents like this."

"My brothers?" said Alice perplexedly.

"Didn't you say you had six brothers?"

Alice remembered and was filled with remorse.

"Oh, I was very naughty. I was teasing you."

"Teasing me?"

"All my life I have wished I had brothers. So has Camilla wished she had. So when we were saying she had no family I couldn't help pretending I had. I'm sorry, Dundas. It was quite silly of me."

His light-colored eyes with their enlarged pupils were on her.

"Then you haven't any family?"

"Not in New Zealand. I have parents in England. My father designs airplanes. I'm the only child and a little superfluous to the life they lead. Besides, I don't care for money—not lots of it."

Dundas took the empty glass from her. He placed it carefully on the tray.

"How very interesting," he said. "Airplanes. Well, you do hide your light under a bushel."

"Not mine. Daddy's. I'm a very disappointing daughter, but one has to be the way one is. It's no use to pretend."

"None at all," said Dundas, suddenly brisk. "I think you're entirely right. I admire you more than ever now. But we'll talk of all this again. Just now you're in no state of health for a discussion on behavior or morals or anything else. I've let you talk far too much already. You have to sleep."

Alice lay back thinking that even the bed was velvet. Now she had to make no effort to keep her eyes open.

"You're nice," she murmured. "You're not going to send me away, are you?"

He leaned forward to pat her cheek. "You shall stay as long as you wish. I can assure you—"

His words were cut short by a heavy footstep at the door. Startled into wakefulness, Alice saw Margaretta standing just within the doorway. She had on an old faded blue dressing-gown. Her hair hung lankily about her face. Her expression was even more forbidding than usual.

"I could smell burning," she said shortly. "I came down to see what it was." Her gaze swept over her father and went scornfully to Alice.

"Look how much better Alice is," Dundas said, apparently unaware of his daughter's anger or scorn. "She's quite wonderfully recovered. It was that sleep, of course. The doctor said what she needed was rest. I gave her some hot milk and I was just leaving her to sleep again."

"What's burning, Margaretta?" Alice asked.

"I don't know. That's what I came down to see."

"Oh, that," said Dundas. "I was just burning some old things out of a drawer. I potter when I can't sleep. Good gracious, child, I'm not likely to set the house on fire. Go back to bed."

"Oh," said Margaretta. She lingered a moment as if she were not entirely satisfied. Then, without another word, she turned on her heel and went.

"She has a nervous temperament," said Dundas. "She always has had. Fancy the smell of my old climbing sweater burning waking her. Though I admit it stank. It didn't worry you?"

"No," said Alice. She hadn't smelled anything, she had only heard those slow footsteps that seemed to betoken anxiety, great anxiety that permitted no sleep.

"Then good night, dear. Sleep well. You'll be quite better tomorrow."

"Yes," Alice said. "Thank you."

Dundas switched the light off, and the pink-striped wallpaper disappeared and the moonlight was back across the floor. The door remained open and now she had no nightmares. But her drowsiness had vanished and her headache had come back. She was trying to remember the expression on Margaretta's face as she had stood at the door, trying to remember her tone of voice, trying to tell herself that the girl was only angry and scornful, not afraid. Surely not afraid.

X

A BED MADE FOR an expected guest, a wardrobe full
of clothes, a starving cat, a fur coat locked in a tin
trunk, a blithe diary full of innocent intrigue, a passionate note from a lover, a whispered voice in the
night, a dead magpie. . . .

Those were the airy clues on which she had to base
her uneasiness about Camilla.

She had awakened with her brain clear, her body
cool and rested. It was broad daylight and the sun
was shining. If it hadn't been for that web of bewilderment in ther mind she would have taken intense
pleasure in the glimpse she got through the window
of mountain peaks, white and brilliant above the
intensely green bush. A black fantail was sporting in
the tree just outside her window, poising like a ballet
dancer and flirting the delicate fan of its tail. The air
was alive with notes of music. She lay identifying the
shiver of bells of the mako-mako, the long golden
note of the tui, the twittering of the bush robins, the
cozy purring quality of the wood-pigeons, and occa-

sionally the discordant note in the orchestra, the screech of the drab-breasted kea.

Just as her pleasure in this comfortable pink-striped room was spoiled by her constant apprehension about Camilla, so was the bird song made discordant by the voice of the kea—the kea with his bird-of-paradise colors hidden under his closed wings and death in his cruel beak.

Webster, the magpie, had had a long cruel beak, too. But he had used it for making his quaint uncanny utterances. Indirectly, by giving significance to his remarks, she had been responsible for his death. Dundas said he had been badly pecked in a fight. It was true that wild magpies attacked and killed tame ones. But unless she saw his body she could not believe that her first impression that his neck had been deliberately wrung had not been true.

Even if Camilla had, for some reason, been imprisoned at the Thorpes' they would have had time to shift her by now. They would know, too, that Alice's fantastic story could scarcely be believed. Even gentle honest Dundas had humored her. He had brought her hot milk in the night and told her to go to sleep. As for Felix, he must have attributed her story to the wanderings of delirium, for he had shown no further interest.

Alice resolutely kept Felix's black-browed face out of her mind. She turned her head and suddenly saw, on the dressing-table, one of Dundas' Dresden figures. It had not been there the night before. He must have crept in with it before she was awake, thinking that its delicate beauty would give her pleasure. It did, too. She was conscious of deep pleasure not so much at the full lacy skirt and exquisitely tiny wrists and ankles of the figure as at Dundas' thoughtfulness.

She remembered Margaretta's words that her father liked small women and she lifted her own arm and looked at her little drooping hand and childish wrist. Felix once in a rare moment of praise had said, "With a few more inches we'd make a Bernhardt of you. But you're too miniature for the stage, my sweet. Too miniature for everyone but me."

Now it was just Dundas who admired her smallness. . . .

Still contemplating her upraised arm, Alice was suddenly aware that Margaretta was at the door. She had a tray in her hands, and when she saw that Alice was awake she came and set it on the table beside the bed. She didn't speak. Alice looked at her lowering face and determined not to be intimidated by this mentally immature girl.

"Good morning, Margaretta," she said. "I feel such a lot better this morning. I'll get up shortly, and then I won't have to be a trouble to you any longer."

"Doctor's coming this morning," Margaretta told her briefly. "You can't get up till he says so."

"Oh, he'll let me, I'm sure." She raised herself on her pillows. The breakfast tray, she saw, contained a plate of thick porridge, some toast which had absorbed its butter and gone cold, and a cup of weak tea. Dundas had said that his daughter was a good housekeeper. No doubt he had wanted to encourage the girl. But did he really always have this kind of fare?

Alice made an effort.

"Thank you, dear. I'll just have a little toast. One doesn't get hungry lying in bed."

She saw Margaretta's eyes on the Dresden figure and involuntarily sighed. Margaretta did not approve. That was clear. It was a pity Margaretta's jealous scowl had to spoil her pleasure in Dundas' little act of kindness.

"What time is the doctor coming?" she asked.

"Ten o'clock."

"Then could I tidy myself a little?"

"I'll fix you after breakfast," Margaretta said grudgingly.

Sure enough, half an hour later, she came back with a basin of water and a towel, and a brush and comb. She refused to let Alice attend to her own toilet, saying her father had insisted that Alice wasn't to lift a finger until the doctor came. But Alice privately concluded that Margaretta, the peculiar person, was a little of a sadist. She obviously took pleasure in slapping soap in her eyes, spilling water down her neck, and pulling her hair quite violently with the comb. Alice strove to keep her temper. It was only for this single time. After that she would be able to get up, and never again would Margaretta lay a finger on her. Perhaps the girl meant to be kind. She was overgrown and clumsy, and likely to spill water, anyway. But she might have made some pretense of an apology.

"You haven't ever thought of going in for hair-dressing, have you?" she asked, as Margaretta gave a particularly vicious pull.

"No," the girl answered, the sarcasm of Alice's remark apparently lost on her.

"I had a ribbon somewhere," Alice said. "It keeps my hair tidy."

Margaretta grunted. Of course, she thought Alice was merely frivolous and conceited to want a ribbon in her hair in bed. But she found the crumpled blue ribbon and tied up her curls with a clumsy yank.

"Thank you," said Alice. "I know you don't like my being here, but truly I can't help it for a day or so."

Margaretta looked at her for the first time. Her eyes were suddenly bright.

"You'll go then, won't you? When the doctor says you can."

"Of course I will. Back to the schoolhouse."

A veil seemed to fall over Margaretta's eyes. She turned abruptly away. She had the towel over her arm, and it swung with her movement. Whether it was intention or not, it caught the Dresden figure on the dressing-table and swept it to the floor. Alice gave a little cry of distress. The figure had broken into innumerable pieces.

For a moment Margaretta looked frightened. Then some inner triumph seemed to fill her and she muttered, "Well, that's one less, anyway."

"Oh, it's a shame," Alice said. "It was a lovely thing."

Margaretta glared at her.

"It was an accident. You can't help accidents." She crouched to pick up the fragments. Now Alice was almost sure that she had knocked over the figure deliberately. Did it annoy her so much that Dundas had put it in here? What a funny girl!

"If I hadn't been here in bed your father wouldn't

have brought it in. So really it's my fault."

Margaretta let the pieces fall with a clatter into the waste-paper basket. Over the sound of broken china Alice heard her muttered voice: "You silly fool, why don't you go?"

The doctor was pleased with Alice's progress. He was a small elderly man whose slightly trembling hands did not inspire her with confidence, but on the other hand neither did he make her nervous.

"You've had a lucky escape, young lady," he said. "Believe me, a very lucky one."

"Why?" Alice asked.

"If that blow on your head had been an inch to the right, if Mr. Hill had not found you when he did, if you hadn't a very sound constitution to resist a chill . . . But we live by 'if's,' don't we?"

It was then that the idea came to Alice that she might have been meant to die, either by the falling tree or by exposure. But no one could have made a tree fall on her. That was purely a freak of the storm. If it had been the tree that had struck her, of course . . . Suddenly she was remembering feeling for the handle of the door, and her hand moving in empty air as she discovered that the door was open.

"When can I get up?" she asked urgently.

"Now there's no need to hurry. You're comfortable here. You couldn't do better than have the rest of the week in bed."

"I can't possibly do that," Alice cried agitatedly. "I have things to do."

"Urgent things?" queried the doctor. His eyes had a dim twinkle. He was a nice old thing, but as blind as a bat, as innocent as a daisy. "Mr. Hill tells me that he insists on your staying here until you are quite well. He says you have no immediate need to leave the coast. And Margaretta's a good little nurse. You stay here and be comfortable." He seemed to become aware of Alice's distress and he added, "You may perhaps get up for a little this afternoon if you have no excitement. *No* excitement, remember." He closed his bag and prepared to go. "An aftermath of an illness of this kind is a tendency to get easily distressed. Remember that, and try to keep calm and quiet."

He was very kind, but he hadn't the faintest conception of the impossibility of keeping calm and quiet.

After he had gone Dundas knocked and came in. He was dressed for the glacier. His sweater, a gay canary yellow, was obviously new. He looked square and very strong in his thick clothes and heavy boots.

"The doctor says you're better, Alice," he said. "Isn't that grand! It's a fine day, so I have to be off to work, but I've told Margaretta she isn't to let you lift a finger to do a thing. Now be a good girl."

He came over to the bed and stooped to give her a chaste kiss on the forehead. He smelled pleasantly of shaving soap. In spite of his gray hair he had an appearance of great virility.

Alice's tired blood gave a faint stir of response. She was being petted and fussed over and it was wonderful.

"Did you get my small gift?" Dundas was looking around inquiringly.

Alice answered remorsefully, "You mean that beautiful little figure? I'm so sorry, but Margaretta and I had an accident.

She saw the anger in his face as he said, "You mean Margaretta had an accident. Margaretta's clumsiness—" Then he recovered himself. "I suppose it was only an ornament. But I have a feeling for those small things." His eyes rested on her thoughtfully. ("You're small, too," they were saying. . . .) "I wanted you to share them," he said. "But never mind. There are others."

The moment he was out of the room Alice sprang out of bed. Margaretta, for all her callousness, had at least had the thought to bring things over from the schoolhouse, and Alice found her own dressing-gown hanging in the enormous wardrobe. She put it on, and when she had heard Dundas' car start up and drive away she went cautiously downstairs. There seemed to be no one about. A cool mountain wind blew through the open doors and windows. The telephone was in the hall. Now was her opportunity to pick it up and ring the police at Hokitika. What would she say? "A friend of mine is missing under suspicious circumstances. I suspect the people living at the Glacier Farm, a Mr. Dalton Thorpe and his sister. Will you come out and investigate?" Her hand was almost on the telephone. But at the last minute something stopped her. It was the memory of Webster lying dead in her hand, and of Felix's voice saying, "Confound you, tell me what you know."

Supposing it had been Felix who had been afraid of Webster's inconsequential chatter. . . .

Suddenly Alice felt very weak and tired. A grayness came over her. Nothing seemed to matter, not even Camilla. She walked into the dining-room and sat in one of the big leather chairs and closed her eyes. Why didn't she take Margaretta's advice and go away? There was only one person who genuinely wanted her here and that was Dundas. Dundas was falling in love with her, she was afraid. Was it fair to let him do that? He saw her as an ornament to his house, an animate figure among all these lovely in-animate ones that stood like small frozen ghosts around the room. He was giving her the same loving care as his Dresden ladies.

But it was pleasant to be cared for. In her present state of mind it was extremely acceptable. She was content for this state of things to go on indefinitely, in spite of Margaretta's hostility.

With Margaretta's name in her mind she was sud-denly conscious of Margaretta's voice speaking to someone somewhere in the house.

"No, I'm afraid you can't see her. The doctor said she wasn't to have any visitors."

The statement was made in Margaretta's usual un-gracious tones. It would not be that she was protect-ing her, Alice thought cynically, but that she was taking pleasure in being obstructive.

"Then when will I be permitted to see her?" The voice was Dalton Thorpe's clipped impatient one.

Alice felt a wave of dizziness come over her. She had an impulse to creep out of the room and run upstairs to the safety and privacy of her bedroom. But to get to the stairs she had to cross the hall, in full view of whoever stood at the front door, and, any-way, she had run away once too often. If she had

129

remained at the Thorpes' the other night she would not be here ill, and she might have discovered the secret to the whole mystery. If nothing worse than a practical joke had been played on her . . .

Her head lifted high in the impotent desire for more inches, her characteristic pose in times of stress, Alice walked into the hall.

Margaretta was just saying unhelpfully, "I wouldn't know when she'll be allowed visitors," when Alice said brightly:

"Good morning, Mr. Thorpe. What was it you wanted to see me about?"

Margaretta stepped aside in surprise, and Alice could see Dalton Thorpe's long narrow face with the close-set eyes that could be implacable, cruel. . . . She could imagine him in the robes of the Inquisition. How, she wondered, could Camilla have had the courage to trifle with a man like this?

Dalton looked at Margaretta inquiringly. Margaretta shrugged her shoulders and walked away. Dalton came into the hall and looked down at Alice.

"Ah, Miss Ashton, I'm glad to see you well again."

But he didn't seem to be overcome with pleasure. Indeed, his cold eyes and down-turned lips could have been disappointed.

"I'm all right," said Alice briefly. "I suppose you want to know why I left you so rudely the other night."

"The fault was mine for those punctured tires," he answered with perfect courtesy.

It suddenly occurred to Alice that the punctured tires could have been a story told to keep her there while Dalton took the car and went to search Camilla's cottage for any other incriminating evidence and to kill poor innocent Webster. It could have been Dalton behind that open door. Why hadn't she thought of that before? The idea seemed so feasible that Alice found herself actually shrinking back from Dalton as if his hands were threatening her in the darkness once more.

"Did you get them mended?" she asked wildly.

"Naturally." He gave a quick turn of his head, almost as if he thought someone might be eavesdropping. Then he said, "My sister was very upset about the whole affair. In fact she has been in bed ever since. She has poor health at the best of times."

"I'm sorry to hear that," Alice said politely. (Didn't it occur to him that she had been ill herself and at this minute was on the point of collapse?)

"She asked me to inquire from you what upset you. Camilla Mason's rather callous behavior worried her a great deal, and now she feels she would like to have some explanation for this."

"I wonder where Camilla is," Alice said idly. "Do you know that someone came to me in the night at your place and said 'Camilla's here'? Wasn't that silly?"

She looked at him with innocent eyes. He moved the tip of his tongue over his lips.

"Extremely silly. So silly that I suggest you were dreaming."

"Perhaps," Alice agreed. "But one would hardly dream one's hair was tied to the bedpost."

A curious look flickered in Dalton's eyes. It might have been guilt or anger or fear.

"What an extraordinary thing to say, Miss Ashton. You had a ribbon on, hadn't you? Surely it must have got caught around the bedpost. Or again, may I suggest that you were still dreaming?"

"Not this time," said Alice pleasantly. "I don't get panicky over a dream. And I admit I did get panicky over this. It was childish of me, perhaps. But I did."

"Camilla's disappearance has made you nervous," Dalton said. "In the middle of a dark and stormy night things become distorted. I suggest you had this on your mind and had a bad nightmare. In any case I hope you won't hold it against us that this happened in our house."

He was so smooth and suave, no one was going to believe her fantastic story against his calm considered explanation. Even the police would laugh at her. Perhaps what he said was true. Perhaps she had been dreaming.

All at once she wanted to believe that it had all been a dream. That was much the easiest thing to accept. She was too weak and tired to hold on to her difficult courage, to fight against this man with his smooth manner and hypnotic eyes.

"I don't hold anything against you," she murmured. Now faintness was really creeping up on her. She put her hands against the wall behind her. Dalton's face seemed to come very close. It swelled and receded and swelled again.

"If you did, I might be obliged to take steps."

Had he really said that? She couldn't be sure because her eyes were playing tricks on her. She thought he was adjusting a ruffle at his throat. His

hands, wavering before her eyes, were exaggeratedly long and thin. "I should be sorry to do that."
His voice was fading away. . . .

XI

SHE WAS LYING on the shiny leather couch in the dining-room. Margaretta was bending over her with a glass of brandy in her hand.

"Take a swallow of this," she was saying. Now her voice was not unkind. It was brisk and cool and business-like. It was a voice one obeyed. Alice raised her head and obediently sipped the brandy. The room came slowly back into focus. There was the cuckoo clock and the glass chandelier and the Satsuma bowls and the Dresden figures. Alice began to count the pale ladies in their petrified attitudes. One, two, three, four, five, six—she had thought there had been more—oh, there was one on the top of the bookcase. Seven. . . . What was the terror she was trying to keep out of her mind?

"I told Mr. Thorpe you weren't to have visitors," Margaretta was saying. "If you hadn't been downstairs I wouldn't have let him see you. And now, you see, you're worse again. We had to lift you onto the couch."

"Did—Mr. Thorpe—carry me?"

Margaretta permitted herself a faint smile.

"He got a fright. Serve him right, keeping you there talking. I suppose he's afraid of his precious reputation, having a guest leave his house in the middle of the night.''

Alice met Margaretta's shrewd eyes.

''As a matter of fact he is. I think he hopes I won't talk.'' (*I'll have to take steps....* What kind of steps? Had Camilla once talked unwisely?)

''That would be too bad, wouldn't it?'' said Margaretta contemptuously. ''We haven't much time for him and his sister. They think they're just too exclusive for the valley. Well, why do they live here, then?'' She paused and said curiously, ''But why *did* you leave there so suddenly?''

''They were playing tricks on me. He says I dreamed it. I couldn't have. Really, I couldn't.'' She thought of that endless walk in the storm and sighed. ''Everyone seems to want me to go away from here.''

Margaretta's young face suddenly had the grim lines of a jailer again.

''That's true. You ought to take the hint.''

Alice said wistfully, ''Margaretta, you were kind a minute ago. Now you're being horrid again.''

The girl flushed. She turned away abruptly.

''I wasn't kind. It's just that I like nursing. But you're better now. And I'm telling you, whatever my father might say, it's better for you to go away.''

''I'm getting tired of this,'' Alice said. ''What harm am I doing? Is it something to do with Camilla?''

Margaretta swung around. Her face was flushed and piteous.

''I don't know,'' she mumbled. ''I don't know.'' And quickly she went out of the room.

At half past four that afternoon the bus roared past. The capricious weather had changed again, and clouds had gathered low on the mountains. Margaretta, still maintaining the aloof silence she had kept since their conversation that morning, had unbent sufficiently to light a fire, and Alice had settled down gratefully by its warmth. She was impatient with herself for still feeling stupidly weak and shaky. She wanted to go back to bed, but stubbornly would not give in. She was determined to stay up until Dundas came home, and for that reason she had newly brushed her hair and put on lipstick. Whatever her private state of mind was, she looked as cozy as a kitten when Felix walked in.

She hadn't heard Margaretta speak to him in the hall. She hadn't known anyone was there. She looked up and he was standing over her. From habit her heart gave that great jump that was mingled delight and panic. Before she knew what she was saying the words were off her tongue.

"Felix, did you steal the diaries? Did you kill Webster?"

From a great height he answered her: "Did you think that one up or did someone put the idea in your head?"

"Of course no one put it in my head. But there was Webster dead, and the night before you had been trying to make him talk. I heard you."

Felix squatted down beside her on the hearthrug. His black brows were drawn together. All the merry light had gone out of his eyes.

"When I came to see you two days ago," he said, "you talked a lot of nonsense to me, but I forgave you because you didn't know what you were saying. Now you do know what you are saying and you think this. All right, Alice, think what you will. It makes no odds to me. I've told you to go away, but I can see you are much too comfortable. I can only leave you to it."

He was so near to her. She cared nothing for him any longer. But she hated to see the way his eyes had grown hard and contemptuous.

"Felix, I couldn't travel while I was ill."

"Granted you couldn't, but what about now? Are you going to let me book a seat for you on the bus tomorrow?"

Alice thought of Camilla's little cottage with its air of mystery, of beautiful unhappy Katherine Thorpe and her queer threatening brother, of surly Margaretta, of Dundas with his gentle passion for small women, and like a fantastic backdrop on a stage the mountains, the lowering clouds, the white frozen stream of the glacier.

"No," she said definitely. "It's much too interesting here. Anyway, I refuse to be ordered about like this. I'm getting much too tired of people telling me to go away. I'm not spilling their little schemes—whatever they are."

Felix regarded her in his assessing way.

"Is it only a passion for drama that keeps you here, such as long midnight walks and trees hurled at you in storms?"

"You mean, don't you, is it Dundas Hill who keeps me here? You've told me repeatedly that we're through. I don't ask you questions about what you're doing, so I'm sorry, but it's entirely none of your business whether I'm interested in another man or not."

"Those words have a familiar sound," said Felix thoughtfully.

"Familiar?"

"Yes, Camilla used them to me not ten days ago. I was poking my nose in, as usual."

That sense of disquiet, never far away, was back with Alice again.

"What were you poking your nose into?"

"One of her mysterious intrigues. By the way, it might interest you to know that Camilla was not married in Hokitika."

"Not?"

"According to the marriage register, no. But there are a great many other places where she could have been married. Nevertheless, I may be on to something. A parson in Rutland Street—"

"Well, Alice, Felix!" That was Dundas' hearty voice suddenly breaking upon them. He came striding into the room still in his climbing clothes, his boots muddy now, his skin bright with windburn. "Alice, my dear, it's grand to see you up. Felix, has Margaretta given you a drink? Ah, she's naughty. I'll get you one. But first, news of Camilla. In the mailbag you brought down. A letter for you, Alice, and one for me."

"Where is she?" Alice demanded, springing up and taking the letter. "What does she say?"

"Read your letter, child. Read your letter."

Alice could scarcely believe that the answer to the mystery lay in that slim envelope with its neatly printed address and Australian postmark. She tore it open and took out the printed sheet inside. (Why had Camilla this craze for printing? It must come from teaching it in school.)

DEAR ALICE,

YOU MUST BE WONDERING WHERE ON EARTH I HAVE GOT TO AND WHY I HAVE BEHAVED SO PECULIARLY. IT'S ALL DUE TO REX WHO WAS CATCHING A PLANE TO MELBOURNE AND JUST DIDN'T GIVE ME A MINUTE. I WAS LITERALLY FLOWN TO THE ALTAR! I AM WRITING THIS TO YOU AT THE COTTAGE BECAUSE I HAVE A HUNCH YOU WILL STILL BE THERE. I HOPE ONE OR TWO OF MY IMPORTUNATE FRIENDS HAVE NOT BEEN WORRYING YOU! I HAVE WRITTEN TO DUNDAS TELLING HIM WHERE TO HAVE MY THINGS SENT, PARTICULARLY A FUR COAT WHICH YOU MUST HAVE WONDERED WHY I LEFT. REX JUST WOULDN'T LET ME PACK A THING. I AM TRULY SORRY TO HAVE BEEN SUCH A BAD HOSTESS, BUT YOU KNOW ME. I GET CAR-RIED AWAY, REALLY CARRIED AWAY, HA, HA! WE ARE LEAVING FOR SAN FRANCISCO TOMORROW, AND THEN SOME PLACE IN THE MIDDLE WEST. ISN'T IT EXCITING! REX IS TERRIBLY SWEET. YOU MIGHT FLING A FEW APOLOGIES FOR MY BE-HAVIOR AROUND THE VALLEY, TO THE THORPES, FELIX, ETC. AREN'T I BAD! I HOPE YOU HAVE LOOKED AFTER MY ANIMALS.

LOTS OF LOVE FROM YOUR ALWAYS UNRELI-ABLE

CAMILLA.

Alice read the letter aloud, slowly. When she had finished she felt curiously flat. After what had happened, both in her imagination and in fact, this explanation seemed a tepid anticlimax.

"I can't think why Camilla has taken to this habit of printing. She never used to," she said.

Felix took the letter from her. He perused it slowly, in silence. Dundas said, "Mine was much to the same effect. I must say it takes a burden off my mind knowing where to send her things. I have a new teacher arriving tomorrow, and she will probably like to stay at the cottage until we decide whether to renovate it or pull it down. Well, one likes a neat end to things."

Felix handed the letter back to Alice. He still made no comment. He looked as if he were suffering from a feeling of anticlimax, too. Alice realized that he never had believed in Camilla's elopement, and was finding it difficult to adjust his theories.

She realized that she hadn't believed in it either. There had been so many puzzling things. (How to explain what had happened to her in the Thorpe house, and that voice whispering, "Camilla's here"?) But here was the evidence in her hands, and she could not but be glad for the happy ending. Camilla's luck had held at last.

When Dundas brought drinks and said in his deep pleasant voice, "Now we can drink to Camilla's happiness in all sincerity, and I hope my next teacher is just a little more stable," she laughed and raised her glass contentedly.

Felix, after a moment, did so, too. But he murmured:

> " 'Tis ten to one this play can never please
> All that are here. . . ."

Dundas nodded understandingly.

"Ah, my dear fellow. But may I suggest that with your talents you need never be at a loss?"

It occurred to Alice afterwards that Dundas might have been wrong in supposing that Felix was suffering from jealousy. His careless quotation could have meant that just as he had not believed in Camilla's elopement, now he did not believe in the explanation contained in her letter.

But the letter had a Sydney postmark. It was completely genuine. Alice had studied it a dozen times. It was Camilla talking in her old gay haphazard way. It explained everything, except perhaps the origin of the fur coat. But one would not expect Camilla to give away indiscreet secrets. No, there was nothing more to worry about. Camilla was safe and was going to lose herself in the anonymity of the Middle West. Good luck to her.

Alice was lighthearted as she went upstairs to the bedroom with the candy-striped wallpaper. Dundas had insisted on her having her dinner in bed, and this she was glad to agree to, for the day had been exhausting. But apart from her tiredness she felt better now. The solution to Camilla's disappearance had lifted a great weight from her. Tomorrow she would go back to the schoolhouse and prepare to enjoy her holiday.

As she was undressing, Margaretta came into the room.

"Hello," said Alice. "Isn't it good news about Camilla?"

Margaretta said guardedly, "I suppose it is."

"You don't sound very sure," Alice said in surprise.

Margaretta didn't answer. She had her hands behind her back. Her expression was unreadable.

"Do you?" Alice insisted.

"With Camilla you can't be sure," Margaretta mumbled at last.

Suddenly she brought her right hand out. In it she held a white tissue-paper package.

"Daddy says he's going to have his dinner up here with you," she said in a rush. "You'd better put this on."

She had flushed scarlet with embarrassment, Alice thought, at her first kind action. Alice took the package and opened it. It contained a flame-colored nylon nightdress.

"But, Margaretta!" Alice shook out the delicate flamboyant thing, full of bewilderment. She looked at Margaretta's drab brown dress gaping at its fastenings, and then at this very feminine fastidious garment in her hand. How would Margaretta, who was shamefully shabby and careless about her clothes, come to own a nylon nightdress of this quality?

"It was given to me," Margaretta said, without meeting Alice's eyes. "I've never worn it."

"But you mustn't lend me a pretty thing like this that's never been worn," Alice protested. "You keep it for—"

"For what?" Margaretta asked roughly. "You can imagine me in nylon."

"Yes, but—"

"Wear it!" Margaretta ordered. "It's better than those old cotton things of mine you've had on. It'll suit you," she added in her blunt ungracious way, and abruptly, so that there could be no more argument, she left the room.

Alice put the nightdress on. That little core of uneasiness was stirring in her again as she did so. But it was a lovely thing. Its glowing color made her whole body a flame. She thought of Dundas coming in presently, and suddenly her uneasiness gave way to excitement and the old feminine desire to light admiration in a man's eyes.

When Dundas came in he was carrying a card-table. He carefully erected it by the bed, saying in a gay boyish voice, "I'm going to have my dinner in here with you if you'll allow me."

Then he looked up and saw her.

It was curious how the pupils of his eyes expanded as she watched. Like a startled cat's, like a tiger's. Why should Katherine think his eyes were like a tiger's when the rest of his face was so bland and genial?

"Why—you're all dressed up."

Had he never seen an attractive woman in bed before? Alice knew that she looked extremely attractive. She had the ribbon coquettishly in her curls and weakness had made a brilliant spot of color in either cheek. Her breasts were delicately round beneath the soft smooth texture of the nightdress. It had been fun prettying herself up like this, with Margaretta's unexpected encouragement and the knowledge that Dundas would be coming up to say good night.

But now she wasn't quite so sure. She had an odd feeling that the darkness in his eyes wasn't all admiration.

"This is Margaretta's," she said, indicating the nightdress. "She insisted on my wearing it. It was so kind of her. It's really a little glamorous, isn't it?" She watched his face, and suddenly guessed the reason for his tension. Of course, he was wondering where his prim and quiet daughter had got a luxurious garment like this.

"I don't know where she got it," she went on, "but I'm sure it was in a perfectly legitimate way. You're not worrying about it, are you?"

Suddenly she added, "It's not Camilla's like those shoes were, is it?"

He gave himself a small jerk.

"If it were I wouldn't know." Then, in apology for his abruptness, he said, "It's just that you look so extremely beautiful. But I'd better have a word with Margaretta, all the same. She might be a dark horse, my daughter, eh?"

He was smiling and the tension was past. He went out of the room and Alice lay back thinking idly of the luxurious tastes of the women on the coast: Katherine Thorpe's model evening gowns, Camilla's squirrel coat, Margaretta's nightdress. It was almost as if the thing were infectious, as if it might all stem from one source. She wondered why that thought came to her.

Dundas was gone a long time. Once Alice thought she heard voices raised to a high pitch. But she wasn't sure. The wind was rising again, and a couple of keas were squabbling on the roof. She could hear their shrill profane voices and the scrabbling of their claws on the iron. And suddenly she was thinking of Webster lying in the rain with his poor twisted neck. Whatever Camilla's letter explained, it did not explain why someone should want to kill Webster.

She was sure there was something about the letter of Camilla's that should have been significant, but could not identify what it was. Was it that Camilla had taken to this extraordinary habit of printing? She had never used to do it in letters, but on the other hand Alice had so rarely exchanged letters with her that she could be no authority on her handwriting habits. Nevertheless there was something about that letter. Alice reached over to get it from the bedside table, and the thin substance of the nylon moved against her skin. It had the coolness of flower petals. Out of nowhere, as if the words were spoken aloud, she heard Margaretta saying, *Daddy likes women's clothes.*

The door opened and Alice shot around.

"Did I startle you?" came Dundas' voice. "I should have knocked, but my hands are full, as you see."

He was carrying a tray laden with china, cutlery, a sherry decanter and glasses, and a vase of yellow roses. He put the roses carefully in the middle of the table and turned with his pleasant beaming smile.

"There. A little celebration, you see."

"What are we celebrating?" Alice asked guardedly.

"The good news of Camilla. And your recovery, of course." His eyes rested on her. His voice had its deep velvet quality. "Especially your recovery."

He began setting out the dishes with a deliberation that was almost absentminded. What was he thinking about? Alice wondered, uneasiness stirring in her again. His eyes still had that alert darkened look although he smiled so kindly. *Daddy likes women's clothes*, she was thinking. He took the stopper out of the decanter and with precision filled each glass until the golden liquid reached the brim.

The reason for his deliberation, Alice suddenly noticed, was because his hands were shaking.

"There you are, my dear," he said, handing a glass to Alice.

A drop of the sherry spilled on the bedclothes. He was exaggeratedly upset, getting a table napkin to wipe it up.

"I'm a little nervous," he said. Then he added abruptly in his prim old-fashioned way, "Do you think when one is over forty one should no longer be romantic?"

"Not in the least," Alice answered sincerely.

"I'm forty-two."

He looked so anxious and nervous and distressed that Alice had to help him.

"And what are you romantic about, Dundas?"

"About you, my dear." The words were out now. Dundas took a deep swallow of sherry and went on more boldly, "I've fallen in love with you. I never thought I would fall in love again. In fact, I never have in this way before. I'm hoping very much that I can persuade you to marry me."

"Why, Dundas!" Alice murmured. She should not

have been startled, because Dundas' actions had obviously been leading up to this. But she found it curiously embarrassing to be proposed to as she lay in bed in a borrowed nightdress.

Yet why should she be? Dundas was so kind and gentle and thoughtful. She need never be embarrassed with him. She could just let herself be wrapped in his loving care. She could have what she had longed for all her life, someone to love her deeply and sincerely. There need be no more lonely struggling, no more hardening herself to rebuffs. In a house full of miniature ladies she could be the animate one, set on a pedestal and revered.

Was she wrong to read all that in Dundas' intense gaze?

"What are you thinking?" he asked urgently. "What goes on in your mind? Tell me quickly!" Then, forsaking his modest old-fashioned courtesy, he cried, "Alice, you are my ideal woman! I never thought I would meet her. One so seldom does realize an ideal. But here you are and I'm crazy for you."

As Alice, struggling with her thoughts that held a picture of a mocking jeering Felix, looked at him dumbly, he went on more soberly:

"You're wondering about my first wife. She was a fine woman, but marriage is a thing that sometimes catches one almost unawares when one is very young. I married her when I was only twenty-one. I realize I never really loved her. The way I feel about you only happens once to a man."

Alice wanted to see the humorous side of the situation. He was so intensely solemn, this nice little man, and she should laugh at him kneeling now before her like Solomon before the Queen of Sheba.

But she couldn't laugh. The queer thing was that she didn't know whether she was being herself or Camilla as she anwered, "You're so kind. How can one refuse you?"

She was almost sure she would never have answered a proposal of marriage in those words. It was as if Camilla had spoken them. Yet she had not been thinking particularly of Camilla. It was almost as if a similar situation had occurred, perhaps in this room. . . . No, no, that was being fanciful. Dundas' brilliant eyes, filled with the mystery of their enlarged pupils that blacked out the irises, were full of absolute sincerity. It was she, Alice Ashton, she only, whom he had proposed to since the death of his first wife.

I wonder if it's true what they say about Dundas. . . . From nowhere that haphazard comment out of Camilla's diary came to nag at her.

But her words were spoken now, and Dundas had got eagerly to his feet and was bending over her to kiss her. For one frantic second she had a feeling of suffocation. Then she let his lips press on hers, and she put her arms around her neck and closed her eyes to shut out the picture of a jeering Felix.

She visualized her future reaching, soft and cushiony, before her. She would be mistress of this tall old house, mistress of the duster that attended to the daily requirements of the Satsuma and Cloisonné bowls, the Venetian glass, the Georgian silver and

the little Dresden ladies. She would help Dundas
with his photography, she would learn to go up the
glacier with him beneath the towering snowpeaks.
She would dress on Saturday nights to dine at the
hotel, and smile with complete confidence at Dalton
Thorpe and his beautiful sister. As Dundas' hungry
lips pressed on hers she was seeing all that with the
speed of a dream. There was not time to think of the
ultimate obligations of a wife before Dundas at last
lifted his head and murmured intoxicatedly, "Ah,
darling, darling!"

Alice moved worriedly and pushed him away.

"Before we make decisions, Dundas, what about
Margaretta? She doesn't like me particularly, and I
admit it's difficult for a girl of her age to be suddenly
inflicted with a stepmother not much older."

"Margaretta will be all right," Dundas said confidently. He nuzzled his lips against her neck. "Ah,
my tiny beautiful darling."

"No, Dundas, you must think about this. Margaretta—"

"I have thought about it. Margaretta was very
fond of her mother and has always been afraid of
anyone taking her place. Since her mother's death
she has tranferred her affection to me, and I am the
object that inspires her jealousy." In his stilted language he went on, "That's understandable, and it
explains her hostility to you. But I have just made
her a promise, and you'll see when she comes up that
she'll be quite different."

"What did you promise her?" Alice asked curiously.

"I told her that I was going to ask you to marry me, and if you consented I would allow her to study to become a doctor, as she has always wanted to." He twinkled happily. "She will be overjoyed at our news. Even I will be cast aside now."

XII

IT APPEARED THAT Margaretta had had a passionate wish to study medicine ever since she had been very young. It was true, as Dundas had said, that her antagonism for Alice seemed to have left her, but now there was some other emotion in her eyes. It was not enthusiasm, and it was not excitement about her own longed-for dream coming true. Rather, it was pity. *Could* it be pity? She was an incomprehensible person. It seemed one could never find out what really went on in her mind. Alice only had a feeling of remorse, and a little humiliation, that Margaretta had had to be bribed to accept a stepmother.

Dundas had brought her in and warmly told her the news, and then had left her with Alice. He had gone out of the room confidently, sure that his future wife and his silent awkward daughter were going to make friends. But Margaretta would say nothing except her stiff polite, "I hope you will be happy."

She knows, Alice thought uncomfortably, *that I'm not in love with her father. I'm very fond of him, certainly, I admire and like him, but Margaretta knows I've slipped into this because I'm tired and want security. Even perhaps that I've been tricked into saying yes by some influence that I don't understand.*

She tried to joke.

"I'm really afraid it was this lovely nightdress that precipitated things," she said.

"Yes," said Margaretta. "It would be." She spoke with complete finality, and yet there was an innocent childlike look in her eyes as if she had no conception of the effect of sex on a man's behavior. If she misinterpreted Alice's remark, then there must be another reason connected with the nightdress.

Suddenly Alice was impatient with herself for all this tortuous thought. Why couldn't she simply accept things as they were? If she accepted Camilla's first letter for the truth she would have saved herself a great deal of worry and doubt. She would have saved herself that wild flight from the Thorpe house because of a practical joke, and in turn have avoided that painful accident that had brought her as an invalid here.

But now she was remembering Dalton Thorpe's low threatening voice: *I shall have to take steps. . . .*

"I suppose concussion tends to make one a bit nervous and apprehensive of things," she said tiredly, scarcely aware that she was speaking aloud.

That exasperating pity flickered again in Margaretta's eyes.

"Yes. It affects one's whole nervous system. Nerves are the cause of far more illnesses than most people would believe."

"How long ago should you have been at university, Margaretta?" Alice asked.

"A year. Daddy thought medicine an unsuitable career for a woman. Anyway, he couldn't very well manage without me. But now—"

"And you wanted me to go away," said Alice. "You really did, didn't you? I thought you must be awfully jealous."

"I wasn't what you thought," Margaretta muttered.

"Well, never mind," said Alice, feeling she couldn't bear any more complicated statements that night. "You must let me come to town with you and help you buy clothes. You'll need a lot of things, because really you are rather shabby. You will let me, won't you?"

"Well—all right."

"Good. One day next week, perhaps. If it comes to that I'll have to get things myself. Shall I have a white wedding?"

Downstairs the telephone was ringing, and before Alice could dwell on the unreality of a white wedding or any wedding at all in this wet green stormy country Dundas called that she was wanted on the telephone.

"It's Dodsworth," he said. "If you don't feel like coming down, love, I'll tell him to ring in the morning."

"No, no, I'll come down."

The descent of the stairs made her breathless. Too much was happening, too much. Now Felix ringing, as if he knew of her faithless action. How silly that she should feel this guilt.

She picked up the receiver and said, "Hello," in her breathless voice.

Dundas was standing a little way from her, solicitously. Would he stand there all the time?

"Hello, little Alice." Felix's voice was gay and caressing. He hadn't called her that, or spoken in that tone of voice, for so long. What had happened?

"Hello, Felix. What's wrong?"

"Nothing at all. Are you going back to England?"

"No. I thought you definitely understood all that."

"I underestimated your stubbornness. You're so like a little soft lamb, I didn't think you could be so stubborn."

"Felix, have you been drinking?"

"No, only Dundas' whiskey to toast Camilla. Lucky Camilla. Supposing we call on her in Sydney."

"But she's going to America."

"She didn't say when. She may still be in Sydney when we arrive."

"Felix, what *are* you talking about?"

His gay warm voice, that she had forgotten how much she loved, came over the wire.

"I gave you quite a long time to decide you had better go back to England, because it's really more fun having some cash. But you seem to be quite sure you can get along with practically none, so I thought we'd better get out of here and go to Australia. I may still have to do a spot of bus driving over there, but Charlie Ross writes saying they're forming a company to tour the big cities. Doing Shakespeare and

Shaw. It sounds right up our alley. Don't you agree?''

Alice licked her lips. Dundas had moved into the dining-room and was standing looking broodingly at one of the Dresden figures, no doubt seeing in its static limbs the image of her own. Dundas, with his ideals, his kindness, his longing for her.

But if only he would go out of earshot while she explained to Felix. . . . If he were not in earshot she could not have said what her words would have been, but the knowledge that he was there held her in that peculiar spell that made her speak almost without her own volition.

"Felix, I can't. Much as I would like to—to be in the plays, I mean—I can't."

His voice subtly changed. It was still friendly but now it had a hint of contempt to come.

"What have you done that is as serious as that?" he asked.

"Felix, Dundas—Dundas wants me—"

"Don't we all?" His voice was definitely colder, harder. She was overwhelmingly conscious of Dundas' presence, of his listening ears.

"Felix," she said with a trace of desperation, "Dundas has asked me to marry him and I have agreed."

For a moment or two it seemed as if Felix might have walked away from the telephone. But presently he said heartily, "You *do* surprise me. Congratulations! Congratulations, indeed."

If one hadn't known him so well one would have thought his voice was genuinely hearty. One would have not have been conscious of the subtle undertones of contempt that were meant to hide his intense hurt. Felix thought he could behave to women as thoughtlessly as he pleased, but when a similar thing happened to him he was ridiculously sensitive. Perhaps the male ego was greater, Alice told herself desperately. Perhaps that was all it was.

"Thank you, Felix."

"Then Australia is off?"

"I'm afraid so." No regret sounded in her voice, did it? It mustn't, because of the two pairs of ears listening.

"Well, well!" Felix ruminated. "Both you and Camilla in one week. It's quite overwhelming."

The mention of Camilla stiffened Alice's resistance to his mocking blandishments. She remembered, too, his tendency to telephone attractive girls, and she succumbed to the temptation to be a little petty.

"I agree you must find it so. But there's still Katherine."

"Katherine?"

The innocence in the upward inflexion of his voice could only be assumed.

"She's on tiptoe with anticipation. Don't disappoint her, will you, Felix dear? Don't confine your attentions to the telephone."

"I haven't the least idea what you're talking about. The only time I have telephoned Katherine Thorpe was to inquire if you were there. But let it pass. To change this enthralling subject, did you notice anything odd about that letter of Camilla's?"

The cold finger of apprehension was on her again.

"No. What?"

"Do you know that never in her life has she called me Felix. Isn't it odd that she should do so now?"

Of course in her diary it had always been Dod. *Dod says he would kill me if I play fast and loose with him.* . . . Was that the significant thing about the letter of which she had been half aware?

"Perhaps she had never written to you before," she suggested.

"I admit she hadn't. By the way, does it occur to you the hotel here has a very transient population? Someone could have been leaving for Australia a day or two ago and obligingly taken a letter to post." He paused a little. Then, "Well, never mind. But if you're in Hokitika in the next week or so you might be interested to call on that parson in Rutland Street. The Reverend Adam Manners. He said Camilla called on him the day she failed to come home. He said she was tentatively inquiring about marriage arrangements. She was going to be living at the glaciers, she told him. In her naïve romantic way she was wondering whether to have a white wedding. . . ."

XIII

THAT NIGHT THE three men trooped through Alice's dreams. Dundas saying in his deep caressing voice, "My beautiful little darling!" Felix leaning over her hissing, *"Thou wretched rash intruding fool!"* Dalton Thorpe as thin and attenuated as a ghost making his mysterious threat, "I shall have to take steps."

In between her dreams she lay awake staring at the dark ceiling and wondering why this house suddenly seemed as hostile as the Thorpes'. At intervals the voice of the cuckoo clock, a comic little ghost trying to get some fun out of his haunting, sounded. Rain beat softly on the window. Everything was muted, even, when they began, the slow footsteps overhead.

Dundas' sleepless footsteps were somehow the most disturbing of all.

What was it that he had been burning the previous night? Why sort out things in the dead of night if they were innocent articles that Margaretta or anyone could see? Did he have to hide something from the gaze of his future wife?

No one, she thought, as she at last awoke, could feel less like a girl who had just had and accepted a proposal of marriage. But it hadn't been her voice that had answered that proposal; it had been one that had come to her for no reason. One from her instinct to act, perhaps, or from the queer compulsion she had when she was in this house to be Camilla. But Camilla hadn't been going to marry Dundas. If she had been going to marry anyone in the valley it would have been Dalton Thorpe. Was it for him that she had discussed a white wedding? And then had this American come along and swept her off her feet with the prospect of a glamorous future? Dalton would be a man of such intense pride that he would never admit he had been jilted. He would make great efforts to prevent such information getting out. That could be why he had made those peculiar threats.

But the thing remained: she was lying in the house of her future husband, and presently he would be tapping at the door and calling possessively, "Good morning, darling!" And there would be discussions about the wedding. Dundas would want it to be soon because Margaretta would be going away. And she herself temporarily had no job and very little money, so a quick marriage was a solution to her future.

You little fool! Alice told herself silently. *Here you are with the security and adoration you have been craving, and now you're not happy about it. You're caught in a web of fate. Those could be Camilla's words. But Camilla would extricate herself from any kind of web, where you, you dope, will play honorably.*

The roar of an engine and a sharp honking told her

the bus was approaching. She leaped out of bed and stood with her face pressed against the window watching, down the dahlia-bordered drive, the bus going past. It was too far to see Felix waving his farewell. The honks sounded derisive, as if they were saying, "You've asked for it, so now we leave you to your fate." She didn't even know if he were coming back on another trip, or if he left tonight or tomorrow for Australia. He had asked her to go with him, not because he still loved her, but because he had a conscience about her.

That was what Alice told herself fiercely as, in company with the trickling rain down the window-pane, the tears slid down her cheeks. Felix was gone, leaving her to the gentle suffocation of Dundas' love.

Someone was singing. She had not realized what silent house this was until there was this unaccustomed sound. It was Margaretta singing loudly and curiously defiantly as she went with a mop down the passages.

She paused at Alice's door and said, "I wouldn't bother much with the rooms next to mine. They're only storerooms. Daddy keeps his old photographic plates and things in them, and there's a lot of junk. I could never make him throw anything away, and I don't expect you will be able to either. So it just gets dumped and gathers dust up there."

It was as if she were the successful applicant for a job; she was Margaretta's successor, nothing more. And Margaretta was singing because she was escaping. In fact Margaretta was being extraodinarily vociferous, almost as if something were driving her to talk. Once, when she had been a child staying in her aunt's house, Alice had accidentally broken a Ming bowl that her aunt had valued very much. She had been afraid of her aunt and afraid to confess. She had talked tirelessly about everything in her childish world before at last she was worn out and the confession came tumbling out of her. Margaretta, she realized, was behaving in the same way. Margaretta had to talk rather than think. Was there something on her mind other than the excitement of at last realizing her ambition to become a doctor?

"I'll go back to the schoolhouse today," Alice heard herself saying a little breathlessly.

Margaretta lifted her heavy eyebrows.

"Is there something wrong?"

"No. I'm well enough to go back, that's all."

"You shouldn't really be up," Margaretta said judicially. "After concussion you're supposed to rest. You've been up too soon."

Perhaps it was the concussion that made her so jumpy and nervous. Alice found herself snapping at Margaretta. "Yesterday nothing would have pleased you better than if I'd got up and gone. What has made you change your mind so completely?"

Margaretta's slow painful blush spread over her broad face. She gripped the mop tightly and began vigorously mopping down the passage.

"The damage is done now," she said. Suddenly she flung around. "And don't ask me why. I did what I thought I should." Her forehead was creased as if she were going to cry. She moved on rapidly, and at that moment Dundas came up the stairs. His gray hair was ruffled boyishly; his eyes, colorless and placid, had the slumbrous look of a lazy tiger. (Now she was always going to think of his eyes like a tiger's.)

"Good morning, girls. What is Margaretta being heroic about? Do you know, all her life she has had this romantic notion of saving lives. I think it must be the drama of the operating table that appeals to her. Well, chicken"—he gave Margaretta a light pat on the head—"Alice and I wish you well on your odyssey. But you haven't started on it yet, and I think at this moment breakfast is indicated."

As Margaretta, without a word, turned to go downstairs, Dundas took Alice in his arms. Through the thin material of her housecoat she could feel his hands, strong and square, pressing into her flesh, holding her prisoner. Loud in her ears she could hear the derisive honks of Felix's horn and, after that first instinctive stiffening, she forced herself to relax, and to return Dundas' embrace. Dear Dundas, who was kind and who was going to treasure her. . . .

All through breakfast it wasn't herself nibbling pieces of toast and making polite answers to Dundas' conversation. It was a girl in a dream. She said yes and no automatically, and smiled serenely, and all the time behind her dreamy facade her mind was working furiously. She had to eliminate one thing at a time. The most important thing was to get to Hokitika to see that parson whom Felix had talked about. Then she had to go back to the Thorpes to find out what went on there. Tottie was the person to see. Tottie must tell her why she had given that whispered warning to lock her door. She would go in the daytime. There was nothing of which to be afraid while the sun shone.

If those sources yielded nothing then she could make inquiries at the hotel as to whether any guests had left to fly to Australia in the last week or so.

(If Felix suspected that that letter were faked, how could he walk out and leave the mystery unsolved? If the letter were a hoax, then the first one which she had found on Camilla's mantelpiece would be a hoax also, and something serious must have happened to Camilla. And she alone, with her small amount of courage, was left to find it out!)

"I think it's going to clear," Dundas was saying. "I might get some shots after all. When are you coming on the glacier with me, Alice?"

The clouds had parted and a thin ray of sunshine lay across the tablecloth. The birds were starting to sing. Simultaneously Alice felt her spirits rising. She would be able to get out and accomplish something today after all.

"Oh, one day soon," she answered Dundas. "Is it very difficult?"

"Not at all. We'll go up to Defiance Hut, stay there the night and take some shots at sunrise the next morning. I've been intending to do that for a long time."

"What a man says is easy is often astonishingly difficult," Alice observed to Margaretta. "Do you find the glacier easy?"

Margaretta's eyes were on her plate. Her bent face had its closed brooding look.

"I've never been on it," she said.

"Not really?" Alice was amazed. "But haven't you wanted to?"

"Actually that's my fault," Dundas said. "When

she was small I was nervous about her and wouldn't allow her on the ice. It's made her develop a phobia. She imagines the crevasses and can't face them now."

"Are the crevasses bad?" Alice asked.

"Not until you get higher up. Of course, they can give one a nasty fall."

"You haven't told Alice everything, Daddy," Margaretta said.

"No," Dundas was silent for quite a long time. His eyes had their clear colorless look as if his mind were not behind them. But that was a fallacy, for when he spoke his voice was harsh, as if he were reliving an old tragedy. "The reason I wouldn't allow Margaretta on the glacier when she was a child was because her mother died on it."

"Oh, how dreadful!" Alice murmured, shocked.

"She slipped down a crevasse. It shouldn't have been fatal, but by the time one gets equipment to lift a person out—it was shock, mostly. We were with a party, but she had been nervous and got a bit behind. The guide had cut steps, but they're inclined to get rubbed out after several people have gone over them. She slipped. I blame myself entirely. It wasn't her first time on the glacier. But she had always been nervous and was trying to get over it."

Dundas' eyes came back to meet Alice's. They gave an illusion of tenderness, because his mouth was tender. But really they were empty windows, waiting for that dark person to look out.

"I had meant to tell you this, darling. You would be sure to hear it from another source if I didn't."

The words in Camilla's diary were standing in front

of Alice's eyes. *I wonder if it's true what they say about Dundas. . . .* What did they say about him? That his wife's death wasn't an accident? Why did she imagine another person dwelt behind Dundas' kind serene eyes?

"How—how very sad for Margaretta," she murmured. "For you both."

"It's all very long ago now," said Dundas in his gentle voice, "You're not to think of it any more. Do you think, darling, that we might get married in that delightful little church that overlooks the glacier? It has a clear window over the altar giving a magnificent view of the mountains. With that purity outside, and you beside me. . ."

And all the time she would see that poor woman sliding, sliding down the ice-blue depths.

"I have to shop before I can get married," Alice said hastily. "Lots of things—"

"Of course, darling. I'm not hurrying you. I don't mean tomorrow or next week."

"Margaretta has to have things, too." She was chattering now. "We must have a couple of days in town. I thought we might go tomorrow. Would tomorrow be all right?"

"If you feel well enough, my dear."

"Of course I'm well enough. I'm completely recovered. I've never felt better." Of course she was well. If she were not, that treacherous other self who longed for love and comfort was likely to say things she didn't mean, was likely to say meekly, "Yes, Dundas, I will marry you in the church at the glacier as soon as you wish," when all the time what she meant was that she could never never marry him.

If only there were someone to whom she could talk about all this. Suddenly she remembered that Dundas had said the new teacher was arriving at the schoolhouse yesterday. She would go over and make her acquaintance.

It was strange coming back to the little house set damply among the spreading ferns and crackling raupo bushes. She felt as though it were years ago that she had sat in the gloom among Camilla's forgotten clothes and smelled the faint perfume that made her seem so mysteriously near.

There was the gash in the ngaio tree where the branch had come down in the storm. It was reassuring to know that the explanation for the blow on her head at least was true and had nothing to do with the door opening in the darkness behind her.

Her knock at the door was answered by a small erect woman who, with her rimless glasses, small sharp eyes and busy manner, was so typical of her profession that it was laughable. This middle-aged plain-faced woman whose pointed nose quivered at the tip was no Camilla, and for that reason she had an air of security about her that was reassuring.

Here, Alice knew instinctively, was an ally.

When the woman spoke her voice was doubly reassuring.

"Why, what a pretty thing you are! I do hope you're the young lady Mr. Hill told me about."

"I expect I am," said Alice. "But why do you hope that?"

"He's going to marry you, isn't he? He's such a nice gentleman and so excited. So romantic, the pet. I hardly know whether I've come to teach school or to supervise a wedding. I'm Letty Wicks, as you will have guessed. But do come in. All your things are here. Are you going to stay with me till the wedding? Mr. Hill says your home is in England. He hopes you'll remain with him and his daughter. He didn't want me to stay in this house either. Really, it is a disgrace, too! But a schoolteacher's salary doesn't run to hotels, and I understand the last teacher made this place quite habitable. What a romance that was! The kettle's boiling. You'll have a cup of tea, won't you? I always have a kettle on boil. It's so friendly, isn't it? And the cat here, poor thing. Tell me, would any woman in her senses go away and leave her cat uncared for?''

Miss Wicks was like a kettle on the boil herself. But her spate of words ceased at last, and Alice, following her brisk figure into the kitchen, was able to say mildly, ''There was a magpie, too. It talked, so it got killed.''

Miss Wicks swung around. The tip of her nose quivered madly.

''My *dear*! What *are* you saying?''

''I found it dead the other night. Dundas said it would been killed in a fight, but I don't agree. There have been too many other odd things.''

''Goodness gracious!'' breathed Miss Wicks. She flung tea-leaves indiscriminately into the teapot and slopped boiling water over them. Her hand quivered almost as much as her thin tender nose-tip.

''As a matter of fact, I knew there was something queer about that woman the way she's left things in school. Her mind just wasn't on her job. I supposed it was on this man she eloped with. Tell me, was his name Dalton?''

Dalton! Why do you ask that?''

''There was a half-finished letter under her blotter. You know, those desk-blotter things. I was starting the new term with a clean piece of blotting-paper, and under the old piece there was this letter. I remember the words exactly:

''DEAR DALTON,

''It's just too generous of you about the fur coat. I don't really think I should take it. After all, I gave you my word—''

''Yes,'' said Alice eagerly. ''Go on.''

''That's all there was. She never finished letter, or else she wrote another and meant to tear this one up. But I hope she married this Dalton if he gave her a valuable present like that. It's hardly playing the game if she didn't.''

''It was gray squirrel,'' said Alice slowly. ''I always thought it was Dalton Thorpe who gave it to her. No, she didn't marry him. And she went away without the coat. That's another thing I couldn't understand. Camilla was usually so mercenary.''

''Goodness!'' exclaimed Miss Wicks. ''Sit down and tell me all about it. Please! I adore a mystery.''

The telling of it brought it all back: the carnation-scented cottage in the rainy gloom; the yellow cat crying and Webster cocking his impudent head; the discovery of the fur coat; Katherine Thorpe's visit; the Thorpes' house, oddly luxurious for such an isolated spot; the punctured tires; the whispered voice in the night; her crazy flight in the storm. She remembered the haven Dundas' house had seemed when she had come back to consciousness, and suddenly her gratitude to Dundas came back, and she was happier, both in her feelings about him and for telling the whole story to a sympathetic listener.

When she had finished, Miss Wicks swallowed her tea in a gulp and said, "Gracious, is this all true? But hasn't Camilla's family been notified?"

"She hasn't any family," Alice said. "She was alone."

Miss Wicks' sharp knowledgeable eyes met hers. An uncontrollable shiver went through Alice. For the first time it came to her that Camilla might be dead.

Then Miss Wicks moved briskly.

"There's my bicycle outside. You get on it and go over to the Thorpes and find out from this Tottie why you were to lock your door. If you ask me, that's the secret to the whole thing."

As Alice hesitated, she blinked her sharp bright eyes and said, "Not frightened, are you? If you encounter Dalton tell him I'm getting in touch with the police if you're not back within two hours. I don't know what the west coast police are like, but a guilty man is allergic to a uniform, no matter what is inside it." She patted Alice's shoulder. "You're a little thing to have to do all this, but there's no one else, my dear. And for the sake of your friend—"

Alice shook the picture of Dalton Thorpe's long medieval face out of her head.

"I know. I meant to go, anyway. I'll be back within the two hours."

"I'll have the kettle on," said Miss Wicks comfortably. "There's nothing like a nice cup of tea."

XIV

THE SUN WAS SHINING and the snowpeaks were a
pure and sparkling white. A break in the low foothills
showed a glimpse of the glacier plunging down like
the bridal veils Camilla had not worn. The air was so
clear that one could see the faint dark marks, like
pencil scribbling, on the ice, which indicated the
deep blue crevasses. Alice thought of climbing up
that frozen surface, stepping carefully in Dundas'
footmarks, following Dundas' sturdy reliable figure.
Had Dundas cried aloud in horror when his wife had
slipped?

Alice resolutely turned her thought from those
things. The exertion of cycling so soon after an illness was making her head a little foggy again. When
she reached the tall white gates leading up to the
Thorpes' house she had a pleasant feeling of being in
a dream. Nothing could harm her because none of
this was real.

She put her bicycle unobtrusively outside the gate
and boldly followed the curving gravel path that led

to the back of the house. All the long windows were shut. There was no sign of anyone about. If she could find the cottage where the servants lived perhaps she could see Tottie alone and slip quietly away again without encountering anyone else.

But there her hopes were disappointed, for on the drying green at the back of the house Mrs. Jobbett was hanging out washing.

There was something peculiarly forbidding about Mrs. Jobbett's strong thick figure and heavy-browed face. Her arms, as she hung up the garments, delicate silks and nylons that were obviously Katherine's, had an almost menacing look. One could imagine her with her fist clenched. It would be like the knotted top of a pruned plane tree.

She turned as Alice approached and surveyed her questioningly. She didn't speak.

"Good morning," Alice said nervously. "I came to see Tottie, if I may. There's a new teacher arrived, and we wanted to arranged about more milk being left."

"You've had your trip for nothing," Mrs. Jobbett said briefly. "Tottie isn't here."

"Not here!" Alice's disbelief sounded in her voice.

Mrs. Jobbett put a peg in her mouth and picked up another garment. It was a nightdress. There were already three nightdresses hanging on the line. So it must be true that Katherine had been ill.

"She's gone back to Hokitika. Didn't like the country. These town girls never do. So you'd better arrange to get your milk somewhere else in the meantime. There's no one here to send."

That statement made, there seemed no way of prolonging the conversation. Mrs. Jobbett either disliked talking or was hostile towards Alice. Alice suspected the latter. It would be because of her rudeness the other night. Seeing Tottie would have been the simple way, but now Tottie was mysteriously unavailable she would have to summon up all her courage.

"Is Miss Thorpe in? May I see her?"

"She's in bed ill and she's not allowed visitors," was the uncompromising answer.

"Oh, I'm sorry." There didn't seem anything else to say. Mrs. Jobbett was like a jailer. Katherine had said she was kept like a prisoner. Why? Couldn't they trust her if she went out? Would she talk too much?

Alice was suddenly aware that Mrs. Jobbett was surveying her with slightly less hostility.

"I hear you've been ill, too. Where do you live? You take my advice and go home. Or at least keep away from here."

"But why, Mrs. Jobbett?"

"I'm just telling you, that's all." She turned back to the clothesline. It was clear she would say no more. She was just the third or fourth person to tell Alice without any explanation to go away. Why was this place so inimical to her? Surely she was harmless.

The danger, of course, existed in her curiosity, her intelligence, and her stubbornly observant eyes. She had to go away before she found out too much. No one wished her, personally, any harm; she was small and pretty and no one would want to hurt her, but if she became a danger she must suffer.

"If it interests you," she said casually, "I'm not going away. Thank you very much for your advice, all the same."

With that same careful casualness she strolled down the path and around to the front of the house. Without hurrying she picked her way across the damp lawn towards the gate. She stopped to smell a rose. It was as if she had called and no one was home and she was regretfully leaving. If Dalton Thorpe should look out at the window and see her he would know that she was not afraid, in spite of his threats.

But her calm was only on the surface. When someone tapped on an upstairs window she spun around as if the tapping fingers were on her own shoulder.

For a moment she couldn't distinguish the figure at the window. Then it moved nearer to the glass and she saw that it was Katherine. She was fully dressed. Her hair was neatly done. She even had a brooch at her throat. She was beckoning violently. She didn't look in the least ill.

Alice took a step towards the house.

"What is it?" she called. Open the window."

Katherine continued to beckon eagerly. Alice could hear her voice faintly.

"Come upstairs, Camilla, come upstairs."

Camilla! Alice froze. Was Katherine mistaking her for Camilla? If she were, Camilla must be here. She must!

"I'll be right up," she called to Katherine and began to run across the lawn. Her excitement had made her forget her fear. She leapt up the steps and put her fingers on the polished doorknob. But it turned without her volition. The door opened and Dalton Thorpe stood within.

"Miss Ashton," he said in his tired cultured voice, "this is an unexpected visit. You sound as if you have been hurrying. You shouldn't do that so soon after an illness."

Alice tried to control her uneven breath.

"Your sister—asked me—to come upstairs."

"I'm afraid my sister isn't allowed visitors." His deepset eyes were not threatening, just dull and immeasurably tired. "I'm sorry. You've come a long way for nothing. Can I give you a drink before you go home?"

"But she was at the window calling me! At least, calling Cam—"

She stopped as his face locked its tight lines. There was a movement behind him as Mrs. Jobbett appeared. He turned his head, and Mrs. Jobbett nodded and went towards the stairs.

"What are you hiding from me?" Alice demanded angrily. "I know that you gave Camilla the fur coat. I found her letter saying so. So if you've got her in this house why don't you tell me? Why don't you ease my mind about her? Don't you realize that I'm terrified she might be dead?"

"I know nothing about Camilla. I wish I did. It's her fault that my sister is ill. She treated her badly and Katherine has taken it to heart. But you mustn't accuse me of hiding her. That's quite untrue."

"Then why is Katherine always suggesting she's here?"

"I tell you, my sister isn't well. We're going to

leave here. I'm sorry to have to do this, but it doesn't suit Katherine's health.''

"Why did you make Tottie leave?" Alice persisted. "Is it because of something she knew?"

She saw then that she had gone too far. She drew back from his dark tight anger.

"I think you are a very rash and impertinent little girl. Will you go away now? Talk to Dundas Hill about Camilla. Ask him your stupid questions. But keep away from here. That's all I ask you to do."

It was humiliating to run away twice, but what else could she do? He barred the way to Katherine, and Katherine was the only person who might tell her anything—Katherine who was kept a prisoner. . . . Alice tried to make her exit as dignified as possible. She forced herself not to hurry down the path. She knew that Dalton Thorpe watched every step she took. She could feel his angry tired eyes boring into her back. Frightened as she was of him, there was something about him that roused an odd sympathy in her. Whatever he had done or was doing, he looked so unhappy.

At the gate she dared to take a last look at the house. The long windows were blank and empty. Did a shadow move across one? If it did it was the heavy square implacable shape of Mrs. Jobbett.

The clouds were coming down over the snow-peaks and the wind was cold. Alice had stopped thinking. She pedaled along like an automaton. All she was conscious of was that at the end of her journey there was Miss Wicks' cheery chatter and her promised cup of tea.

Miss Wicks made her pronouncement immediately. Her small bright eyes snapping, she said, "There's guilt for you, if ever there was. Of course, that's the reason you weren't allowed to speak to the girl. She might have told you something. Where do you think he's put the body?"

Seeing Alice's expression, she was instantly sorry, apologizing profusely.

"I'm so used to reading thrillers, I can't look on Camilla as a real person. But she was your friend. I shouldn't have said that. Of course there won't be a body. But what makes this Dalton Thorpe guilty? Do you know what I think you must do? You must go to Hokitika tomorrow and find where Tottie lives."

This had been the half-formed plan in Alice's own head. She agreed, but added, "I won't be able to go without Margaretta. I've promised to help her shop."

"Well, get rid of her some way for an hour or two. And see that parson, too."

The mention of the parson brought back so vivid a memory of Felix that Alice had to blink her eyes against the quick tears. (*Oh, Felix, what sort of a stupid senseless nightmare are we living in? When will we wake up and find out that it is a nightmare?*)

"And here's a couple of letters addressed to Miss Mason," Miss Wicks was saying. "They arrived today. I don't know whether Mr. Hill will want to send them on or not. Personally, I'd wait until you know something more definite, in spite of that letter. Anyone can print a letter."

Alice took the letters and slipped them into her bag without looking at them. She was thinking that if she were going to Hokitika with Margaretta tomorrow she had better have one last night at Dundas', and they could catch the bus together in the morning.

Miss Wicks was fondling the yellow cat and saying, "How anyone could leave a cat like this to starve I don't know. That's what makes me think the whole thing is so fishy. You should really call the police, but police like something cut and dried, not just airy fancies. You must see that Tottie. She'll tell you something."

XV

ALL EVENING the white house with the girl at the window was a tiny disturbing picture at the back of Alice's mind. It was not fair to Dundas that once again she couldn't concentrate on his conversation. In the middle of his explanation about the use of yellow filters for photographs on snow or ice she said:

"Margaretta and I must go to Hokitika tomorrow."

Margaretta looked up from her sewing.

"No bus tomorrow," she said briefly.

Alice had a moment of panic. They had to go tomorrow. They had to. It was the white house that had been a prison, first for her and now mysteriously for Katherine, perhaps also for Camilla, yet contrarily it seemed that this cluttered room with the friendly cuckoo clock, the small pale figures, the firelight and the shining glass was the prison.

She really was getting neurotic. Because there was no bus and her urgent business must wait another day she was imagining herself being deliberately kept here.

"If you must go tomorrow," Dundas was saying in his slow deep tones, "I can take you. I've one or two things to do myself."

"Oh, can you?" said Alice gratefully.

But instantly her relief left her and she began to wonder how she could search for Tottie with Dundas at her heels all day. She had grown now to feel that she could confide in nobody, not even the man whom she had promised to marry.

Margaretta looked up again, surprise on her face.

"But, Daddy, you went to Hokitika last week. You don't usually go so often."

Impatience flickered in Dundas' eyes. But he answered quite mildly, "What if I did? Life doesn't always run to routine. And if you're getting fitted out for college, I'm getting ready for a wedding. Which I consider much more important." He puffed out his chest with pleased importance. He was a little man still naïvely excited and uncertain about his immense good fortune. He came over to kiss Alice's cheek. "We'll go tomorrow. We'll stay a night at a hotel. Make a do of it."

Alice sat quite still. Even Dundas' kiss did not affect her in any way. She was looking at the picture in her mind, pondering over and over why Katherine should be kept a prisoner upstairs because Camilla had disappeared.

The lights in the chandelier danced like bits of broken glass catching the sun. The silver on the sideboard and the luster jugs and Satsuma bowls caught points of brilliance. If she were to die what relics would Dundas, with his hoarding instinct, keep of her?

The cuckoo popped out of the clock suddenly and gave his pert cry. Alice jumped convulsively.

Dundas laughed tenderly. "You're tired to death, my sweet. Go to bed. We'll be making an early start tomorrow. Take her upstairs, Margaretta."

Yes, I am tired to death, Alice thought. *But I don't like those words. They're like everything here, innocent on the surface only.*

She caught herself up from that wandering of an overstrained imagination and meekly got up to follow Margaretta out of the room.

"I saw Miss Wicks today," she said to Dundas as she went out of the room. "She's nice, but not a bit like Camilla."

Dundas' voice followed her.

"You forget Camilla, darling. You won't see her again."

Margaretta came into her room with her and sat on the bed.

"What are you going to wear for your wedding?" she asked.

"Oh, I don't know. I can't seem to think. I don't think my head is quite better yet. It isn't interested in clothes, anyway."

Margaretta looked at her with her light-colored expressionless eyes.

"Would you like to see what my mother wore to her wedding?"

As Alice stared, she went on:

"Come and see. It's just upstairs in one of the rooms I said not to bother about dusting. Daddy's gone to the darkroom to develop prints. He'll be there for hours."

It was as much as to say that if her father were about Margaretta wouldn't have dreamed of showing Alice the things. Not comprehending what tortuous paths Margaretta's mind followed, Alice obediently went upstairs with her to the small room where, the other night, Katherine had cried excitedly, "Gracious, you are hoarders!" and then had come back with the black suède shoes. Margaretta opened the door of a large wardrobe and showed Alice the line of dresses hanging as they had hung for the last ten years, drooping and dingy with age.

"See," she said. "Daddy could never bear to throw anything away. But it's useless keeping them; they're quite out of date. This was my mother's wedding dress." She pulled out the drawer of an old bureau and disclosed the white satin dress with the conventional spray of orange blossom and the gauzy veil.

An odor of camphor hung about. (*Get mothballs in town today,* Camilla had written, because she had a precious fur coat to protect, not an old-fashioned wedding dress.)

"It really is rather super," Margaretta said. "I suppose Mummy was keeping it for me. Me!" she repeated in her young scornful voice. "Shall I unfold it?"

"No," said Alice rather hastily. She couldn't understand her intense distaste for this room. It wasn't as if she were in love with Dundas. That would have given her reason to dislike looking at her predecessor's clothes.

It was something else, something she couldn't explain, a feeling that there were too many clothes in this affair. Camilla's strewn about the cottage, Katherine's expensive models, Margaretta's mysterious nylon nightdress, and now this rack of dingy garments.

At random she pulled open the lower drawer of the bureau, and to her surprise there lay within, still in its tissue wrappings, another white dress, this time a heavy lace that was going slightly discolored.

"Why, what's this?" she murmured. "It looks as if it's never been worn."

Margaretta had stepped back a pace. Her face had flushed and her eyes had a look of tension.

"Neither it has," she said.

Alice had a curious feeling that she had been meant to discover this dress. It was the reason for being brought up here.

"Whose is it?" she asked sharply.

"It belongs to Miss Jennings," Margaretta said cryptically.

"Who on earth is Miss Jennings? Margaretta, for goodness' sake stop being so mysterious."

"Didn't Daddy tell you?" Now Margaretta's eyes had a wide-open innocent look. "I thought probably he would. She was here about six years ago. She was one of our housekeepers. She was going to marry Daddy. But at the last minute they quarreled or something. She went away and left her wedding dress. Of course, she wouldn't want it when she wasn't going to be married, after all, and I guess she never sent for it because she didn't want to be reminded of what had happened. I found it not long ago, wrapped in newspapers in a suitcase. It seemed a pity if it was to be kept not to look after it, so I put it in here. As I said, Daddy can't bear to throw things away. And they're absolutely useless."

Alice stood quite still. The fact that there had been another woman in Dundas' life disturbed her very little. But the fact that Margaretta had felt it necessary to give her this information did. Margaretta had wanted to get those two stored wedding dresses off her mind. Now she had done so, and it was Alice who had the uneasiness, the little prickles of apprehension running up her spine.

For after all it was Alice who was to wear the third wedding dress.

"Look," said Margaretta rapidly. She held out her hand and displayed ten five-pound notes. "Look what Daddy has given me to buy clothes with."

"That's nice," said Alice mechanically.

"But do you know he's never given me more than a few shillings in his life before? If I've bought anything it's had to be put on an account so he could see it. He's always been like that. I thought it was because we were pretty poor. Yet now he's given me all this money."

"It's nothing to do with me," Alice said uneasily. "You have fun spending it." She added almost against her will, "Why did you think you had to tell me all this?"

Margaretta looked confused.

"It's only fair you should know. Then if—" She stopped and Alice had to prod her.

"If what? What were you going to say?"

Margaretta burst out, "You don't really love

Daddy, do you? Then why did you say you would marry him?''

Alice tried to face her. She tried to make a dignified answer, such as, ''I admire and respect your father and I know I will be happy with him.'' But the rebellious words wanting to slip off her tongue were, ''It wasn't me speaking when he asked me. It was Camilla. She made me say it.''

Margaretta would never understand that. She didn't understand it herself. But she did understand the reason for Margaretta's anxiety.

''Don't be afraid,'' she said gently. ''You'll get away to college. Nothing will stop you. I'll manage your father.''

Margaretta gave a great sigh. Suddenly, for the first time since Alice had known her, her face was young and carefree. It was as if she had passed on her peculiar unspoken anxieties to Alice.

Just before they were leaving the next morning Miss Wicks came panting up to the front door. She asked for Alice, and slipped a scrap of paper into her hand.

''Something I'd like you to get for me in town today, if you don't mind,'' she said. Her sharp eyes twinkled. ''Have a good time, dear. Come and have a cup of tea with me when you get back.''

Alice read the writing on the slip of paper:

Tottie's name is Smale. Her father is a butcher.

It was true, as Felix had said, that she was a silly little brainless lamb. It hadn't occurred to her to seek for information about Tottie here. Rather, she was going to look for a needle in a haystack. It took Miss Wicks' shrewd head to think of those things.

"What does she want you to buy?" Margaretta asked.

"Mothballs," Alice answered at random. It shouldn't be difficult to locate a butcher by the name of Smale in a small town. Alice began to feel excited. Within a few hours she would have the answer to at least one problem. Then, when she had seen the Reverend Adam Manners, she would perhaps have the answer to another. For surely he could give her enough information about the man whom Camilla had meant to marry to make it clear who that was.

XVI

CLOTHES, CLOTHES, CLOTHES! Like a recurring theme in a piece of music they ran through this business. Alice watched Margaretta trying on the green coat again, lingering over it longingly because it was the one she wanted most, but its price was too high for her slender purse. Fifty pounds wasn't so much after all, and already she had bought shoes and underclothing.

She had discovered, or perhaps she had known bitterly for a long time, that her figure in a well-cut garment was good. The knowledge was making her linger over her purchasing, and Alice, for all her good-natured assistance, was growing very weary. Besides, there were the things she had to do privately. It seemed as if she would never be able to escape from both Margaretta and Dundas.

It was only with difficulty that they had persuaded Dundas to leave them to their shopping. They had arrived in Hokitika little after midday, had had lunch at the hotel where Dundas had booked rooms for the night, and then at last they had convinced Dundas that his company for the buying of a girl's wardrobe was not desirable.

It was not raining, but the low gray clouds were like a roof over the ugly little town. Why, wondered Alice, had the small towns in New Zealand such a hasty overnight appearance? They looked as if they had been erected to meet temporary emergencies, such as a gold rush, and then had lingered on, half empty, half dead, a century straining at their shabby timbers. Hokitika was one of these. Its small streets rambled towards the wooded countryside. It was full of derelict hotels and unpretentious shops that were more practical than interesting. It was the last place where one would expect to find smart clothes, but Margaretta seemed content to shop there.

She was so absorbed over her choice of coats (how different she had become from the distressed girl whom she and Katherine had tried to smarten!) that Alice suddenly could wait no longer. Besides, she had to get rid of the girl for a little.

"Margaretta—do you mind?— I feel a little faint. I think I'll go back to the hotel."

Margaretta looked at her concernedly. Gone now was her hostility. She was all friendliness, a nice overgrown girl at last able to throw off her frustrations.

"Oh, I'm sorry, Alice. I've kept you standing around too much. I forget you've been ill. A nice doctor I'll make. I'll come back to the hotel with you."

"No! No, please don't. You have to finish your shopping. You might not get another chance. I'll be perfectly all right out in the fresh air."

"Well—I know Daddy's usually impatient to get started in the morning."

"I'll be quite all right," Alice assured her. "Don't you hurry at all."

She escaped out of the stuffy shop. To be honest, she did feel a little faint, but it was nothing that fresh air would not cure. Out in the street she accosted the first passerby.

"Excuse me! Could you tell me where Smale's butcher's shop is?"

"Just around the corner, miss," came the answer.

"Thank you," said Alice. She hurried around the corner, and there, sure enough, was the small shop with its window full of cuts of lamb and beef. A little man with a round jolly face was hanging a string of sausages in the window. He was the only person in sight, and Alice knew by his appearance that her search was at an end. It had been so simple that it was absurd.

"Yes, madam?" said the man briskly, as she came into the shop.

Alice used no subterfuge.

"Are you Tottie's father?" she asked.

The brisk affable salesmanship in the man's face altered. His eyelids fell over his little round pop-eyes, so like Tottie's that Alice's question had been unnecessary.

"My name is Smale," he answered. "What do you want?"

"I simply want to know where I can see Tottie," Alice said. "I knew her at the Thorpes', but she left while I was ill and we never said good-bye. I just wanted to wish her well."

The man turned back to his sausages.

"She's not here. She left a couple of days ago."

"Left Hokitika?"

"Yes." Alice detected anger and resentment in Mr. Smale's voice. She leaned over the counter.

"Why did she do that, Mr. Smale? Wasn't she happy with the Thorpes? Do you know, I thought there was something odd about that place. I was only there one night, but—well, it wasn't quite the place at which I would have cared to work."

Her ruse succeeded better than she had expected it would. Mr. Smale swung around and demanded in an angry puzzled voice, "What has been going on there? We always thought Tottie was well suited until she comes home with this diamond brooch, and saying she's getting another job in the North Island. Fare paid and all. Now, look, that ain't honest. With some girls maybe there'd be a reason, but Tottie's all right. Her mother and me, we'd swear she ain't done nothing. So why pack her off like that?"

"But didn't Tottie tell you the reason?"

"Not a word out of her," the father said resentfully. "Mrs. Smale was at her from morning to night, but she just kept her mouth shut, and then she packed her bag and off."

Suddenly he realized Alice's potentialities as a witness, and he asked eagerly, "Who are you, miss? Do you know anything?"

"Nothing that would help in the least," said Alice regretfully. "I want to ask Tottie questions. She probably observed what was going on. She knew why a visitor there should lock her door at night. Did you say a diamond brooch?"

"Yes. Only a little bit of a thing, but diamonds, all right. What was it for, miss?"

"I don't know," said Alice slowly, meeting the man's worried eyes. "I think it was probably a bribe. But don't you worry, Mr. Smale. We're going to get to the bottom of this."

"I wish you would, miss. Because one thing Mrs. Smale and I knew. Tottie was frightened out of her wits."

Half an hour later Alice sat in the untidy comfortable parlor of the vicarage in Rutland Street. It had not been quite so simple to find as had Mr. Smale's shop, but she had succeeded in doing so with the help of a friendly taxi driver who obviously thought she wanted to make arrangements for her wedding. As she waited for the Reverend Adam Manners to come in she thought of what Tottie's father had told her. Obviously the diamond brooch had been a bribe to keep Tottie's mouth shut. That was straightforward enough. But somone else had been bribed, too. Margaretta had been bribed with more money than she had ever had. Dalton Thorpe might find it necessary to bribe people because of some dark secret he had, but why did Dundas have to bribe his own daughter? Suddenly a new idea came to Alice. It was possible that Camilla's fur coat had been a bribe, too! Perhaps she had known something. There was that entry in her diary, *Things are getting a bit dangerous.* . . . Could that apply to some outside event and not to her own personal entanglements?

If that were so, Alice thought slowly, then it must have been that the fur coat hadn't succeeded in keeping Camilla's mouth shut. Anyone who knew her would realize that it would only be under the greatest stress that she could prevent her artless chatter. She must have talked. . . .

Why was it, she wondered, that suddenly she so completely disbelieved that letter from Sydney?

Her thoughts were interrupted by an old gentleman with snowy hair cut long and the look of an early saint coming into the room.

"You wished to see me?" he said in a soft mild voice.

As with Mr. Smale, Alice saw no point in beating about the bush.

"I wanted your help in connection with a friend I am trying to trace. I understand she came here three or four weeks ago to arrange for her wedding, and since then she has gone away without leaving any trace."

The old man sat down.

"And if this is so, how can I help you?"

"I thought she might have told you something about the man she was going to marry. If I knew who that was it would help tremendously."

"I think you must be a friend of the young man who came here two or three days ago. A very impetuous young man with black hair. Indeed, he was so imperative that I fancied he must have had a personal interest in this mysterious young woman himself. But now I see you—perhaps—"

Alice dismissed his romantic wandering. The old man was almost in his dotage; it would seem his weakness might be for young couples about to be married. He no doubt gave them long rambling homilies. But being romantic about Felix and her was wasting his time.

"Yes, he's a friend of mine," she said shortly. "He told me to come and have a talk to you. He knows I am very anxious about Camilla. You see, it wouldn't be reasonable if she had arranged her marriage in Hokitika to rush away and be married in Australia. Did she go to great lengths in her plans with you?"

"Oh, very great lengths. She was a very talkative young woman. In fact, I formed the sad conclusion that she was making the mistake of, alas, too many young brides. She was placing all the significance on the pomp of the wedding itself—a pretty but vain show, my dear—and little on the serious side of marriage. Sometimes a girl takes refuge in all the fuss and frippery to hide her nervousness. But I don't think your friend was the nervous type. She was just going to enjoy a little limelight, perhaps?"

Alice could imagine Felix's impatience if the old man had talked to him in this strain. She smiled a little, thinking of his angry brow. Thoughts of Felix would always stir her to tenderness, then to that horrible inconsolable pain. . . .

"Then she had made definite plans for her wedding?" she suggested.

"Oh yes, indeed. It was to be held in my church in the first week in February. She hadn't fixed the exact date and she didn't wish banns to be called, which is a little irregular. She was going to come back and see me, but I'm afraid she never did. And now you tell me she has gone away. Ah, the impetuous child! I hope she will be happy."

Alice leaned forward. Getting information from

this elderly cleric was like penetrating a soft thick mist.

"But tell me, did she ever mention the name of the man she was going to marry?"

"She did, my dear, but there my memory serves me badly. She talked such a great deal. I do remember that she said she would be spending the rest of her life down at the glaciers and that the mountains terrified her—gave her the jimjams was her exact expression." The old man gave his gentle smile. "I thought that she must have seriously contemplated the problems of marriage if she were willing to live in an environment that gave her the —er—jimjams— all the time. Now I seem to remember this name she spoke of. I think it began with a D."

There it was, the vicious circle. It had begun with the letter D and now it had come around to it again. Of course, Camilla might have intended marrying Dalton—or Dundas—or even Felix, her Dod, and then this exciting stranger had come along and swept her off her feet. There was nothing to prove that this hadn't happened.

But why those mysterious bribes that were being made now, when Camilla, to all intents and purposes, was thousands of miles away?

Alice resisted the Reverend Mr. Manner's gentle wistful suggestion that perhaps she would soon be contemplating the state of holy matrimony herself, and came away with the feeling that her head was full of wool.

The only definite sensation that emerged was one of anger with Felix for going away, leaving her to this unsolved problem, throwing her to the wolves. He knew there was much more in it than was apparent on the surface. Perhaps he knew too much. . . . She was suddenly feeling again the limp body of the magpie in her hands, its feathers hard and cold, and remembering Felix's voice: "Tell me what you know, confound you!" Perhaps Felix had thought it wise to disappear. . . . He had issued his formal invitation to her, and then, relieved that she had not accepted it, had gone.

Alice shivered in the gray street, and longed for Dundas. She could no longer think straight (because if Felix had been the man Camilla had intended to marry he wouldn't have told her to go and see that parson and listen to Camilla's flowery plans for a white wedding). She didn't want to think any more at all. She wanted to listen to Dundas saying, "You're tired out, my sweet. You must let me look after you."

It didn't turn out like that at all. When she reached the hotel both Dundas and Margaretta were in the lobby. Margaretta was looking frightened. When she saw Alice she exclaimed in a relieved voice, "Oh, there you are at last. You see, Daddy, I told you she would be here any minute."

"That's right," said Dundas curtly. "Go up to your room and wait for us. I want to talk to Alice."

With an uncertain backward glance—she was the awkward overgrown schoolgirl again—Margaretta went. And Alice, looking at Dundas, saw the dark brilliance of the stranger in his eyes again. Suddenly she realized that he was a middle-aged man, and that she was scarcely older than Margaretta and just as bewildered and frightened.

"Where have you been?" he asked in his curt voice.

"Why, what's wrong, Dundas? I've just been for a walk through the town."

"Margaretta said you were faint and were coming back here to lie down. How could you be walking about the town if you were faint?"

There were people coming in and out, and because they were not alone Dundas had lowered his voice to an angry hiss. It was like a stranger speaking to her.

"I thought the fresh air would do me good. Dundas, you sound as if you're cross-examining me. Why?"

He had the grace to look a little abashed.

"I don't like to let you out of my sight. You're so precious to me. Promise me you won't go off like that alone again."

"But Dundas, that's ridiculous! In a small town like this. Really, if you're going to watch me like that it's no use at all."

"I'm not watching you. It was just that your faintness seemed an excuse."

"Well, if you must know, it was. There was someone I had to see."

Instantly his face was tight again, with a curiously sunken look as if the flesh had been drawn into the deep groove on either side of his mouth.

"Who?"

"Tottie's father. He's a butcher here. I wanted to see Tottie, really, but she's left Hokitika." The mystery of it was sweeping over her again, and she burst out, "Dundas, there's something awfully queer about the Thorpes. They seem to have bribed Tottie to go away in case she talked. There's something she knows. What could it be?''

Had Dundas' face been so tight and wary and strange? Surely she had imagined it, for now he was smiling tolerantly and tucking her hand through his arm.

"Silly little conscientious girl, so you thought you should find out what it was. Actually the facts are that it's absolutely none of your business. I admit you ran into something queer when you stayed there. I admit I've often thought there was something queer about that household. But leave well alone, my dear. Don't go sticking your pretty nose into trouble.''

That bland soothing voice was having its usual magnetic effect on her. Had Dundas really been that angry stranger? Always, after one of those moods of his, she had the impression that it had all existed in her own imagination.

"But Camilla—'' she began.

His brows rose.

"Surely, darling, you're not still worrying about Camilla? We know where she is. I've had her things sent on.'' He began to look uncertain. "Or do you think I'm being a little simple? A little gullible? Do you think the Thorpes—Ah, no, that's fantastic. Come, we can't dwell on morbid ideas like that. We're here to enjoy ourselves. I've ordered a little celebration dinner tonight. I'm afraid the wine isn't very good. You can't get it at these small hotels. But it's the best they have. Run along and rest for an hour, and then meet me down here at seven.''

He pressed her arm lovingly, and now it was as she had expected it to be. She was being absorbed in

Dundas' gentle kindness. But she found it all quite unreassuring. She couldn't think why she had deliberately refrained from telling him about the clergyman and his wandering chatter about Camilla's white wedding.

It was as she came down to dinner that she saw Mrs. Jobbett. The woman was standing in the doorway of the lounge with her back towards Alice. There was no mistaking her squat strong figure, the arrogant masterful turn of her head. She was neatly dressed in black. She looked full of respectablility. She could have been anybody's mother come to have an innocent evening out. But something about her filled Alice with terror. If Mrs. Jobbett were here the Thorpes must be here, too.

Even as Alice hesitated she turned and her hard black eyes rested on the girl standing uncertainly on the bottom step of the stairs. A fleeting look of surprise crossed her face, then she gave a faint smile and said quite pleasantly, "Good evening, Miss Ashton. We didn't expect to see you here."

If the Thorpes were here perhaps she could contrive to see Katherine after all—if she had the courage.

"No, indeed," she murmured.

"You're on your way home, then?"

"No, I'm going back to the glaciers again." Even now Alice found it necessary to defy this woman.

But Mrs. Jobbett seemed to be in an unusually pleasant mood. She nodded and said sympathetically, "I declare I don't know how you can stand all the rain. Gives you the glooms. I can tell you I'm thankful enough to get away."

Before Alice could make any answer she stepped past her and walked purposefully up the stairs. Was she alone, or had she, too, a diamond brooch as a bribe to go away? Alice was debating asking the girl at the reception desk if the Thorpes had arrived, when Margaretta and Dundas came down, and it was too late.

Margaretta wore the new dress she had bought. It made her look grown-up at last. She was a tall young lady, not an overgrown child. But her appearance was ruined by the old childish sulky look that had come back to her face. It was as if she had never been happy, carefree and excited.

Alice sighed. Things were difficult enough without having Margaretta's peculiar brand of contrariness to cope with. She hoped the wine Dundas had promised them would do something to brighten up the girl.

Fortunately Dundas was his affable self again. He ordered a sherry each for them, and then lavishly repeated the order. Margaretta's cheeks were already flushed when they went in to dinner. When she saw the burgundy that the waiter brought with the roast duckling she gave her father a quick glance of perplexity and nervousness. If she was unaccustomed to wine this was going to have an effect on her, Alice thought, sipping her own burgundy and enjoying the warm relaxed feeling it gave her. If she were losing her private fear that Dalton Thorpe would walk in at any moment, then Margaretta must likewise forget whatever it was that troubled her.

Sure enough it was so, for presently, when Dundas had finished a long affable speech about the success Margaretta would be in her new clothes, Margaretta lifted her eyes, now purely defiant, and said to Alice, "When are you going to get your wedding dress?" Suddenly she giggled. "Don't get it too soon, because if you should decide not to marry Daddy it will only be another relic for him."

Dundas' eyes flickered.

"What are you talking about, Margaretta?" he asked pleasantly.

Margaretta giggled again.

"Alice knows."

"I'm afraid my daughter isn't accustomed to burgundy," Dundas said to Alice. "Can you tell me what she is talking about?"

"I expect it's that wedding dress you have upstairs," Alice said. This was a subject she had meant to raise, and, like Margaretta, she found that the wine gave her courage. "Who was Miss Jennings, darling? You never told me about a Miss Jennings."

Dundas picked up the burgundy bottle and refilled Alice's glass.

"What devious tale has Margaretta been telling you, my sweet? If I remember rightly I never discussed the unfortunate matter with her. She was only a child at the time."

"I remember Miss Jennings," Margaretta said in her defiant voice. "She used to have her hair in tight curls, like a little girl. But she really wasn't very young, was she, Daddy? I thought she was quite old."

"Her age had nothing to do with it," said Dundas. He spoke in the controlled voice of someone humoring a child. "Actually she was a little older than me. Perhaps that was one of the reasons why we decided

202

the whole thing was a mistake. I don't remember being particularly conscious that five years or so made a lot of difference, so much as I realized that marriage with her would have been a failure. Fortunately, we both became of one mind on that."

"But how did you come to keep her dress?" Alice asked. Miss Jennings as a person was quite unreal. To Alice she was just a white lace dress going a little discolored and smelling of mothballs. Even had she been deeply in love with Dundas the thought of so inanimate an object as Miss Jennings would give her no uneasiness.

"She didn't tell me where she was going when she left. To be quite frank, she left in rather a state. It was all very upsetting. When I found she had left the dress, naturally I kept it in case she should send for it. But I suppose the whole thing was too painful for her to want to be reminded about it. Anyway, there it is moldering in the attic. I must have a clearance up there. Really I must. You'll think you're marrying a second-hand junk dealer, darling."

Alice smiled dutifully. The thought of her marriage to Dundas was as unreal as the ghost-like Miss Jennings. Margaretta gulped over the last of her wine and looked at her father with her defiant scornful eyes.

And then Dalton Thorpe walked in. He was alone. He stood a moment at the door waiting to be shown to a table. Alice was aware of his quick eyes scanning the room. Then he saw them and without hesitation crossed the room towards them.

"This is fortunate," he said. "I wanted to say good-bye, but I found no one at home when I called.

My sister and I are leaving, you know."

"Leaving!" said Dundas.

Dalton smiled. His face was very pale and gaunt; his eyes had their look of far-off sadness.

"Yes. I told Miss Ashton something of the sort yesterday, but I don't think she believed me."

"But so suddenly!" Dundas protested.

"Ah, Katherine and I do things like that. We decide all at once that we want to move, and off we go the next morning. Actually Katherine always found the mountains a little oppressive. We shall go near the sea, I think. I've left an agent to attend to everything, and we go east tomorrow."

Alice found her voice at last.

"Is Katherine here?" she asked breathlessly.

"Yes. She's not feeling quite strong enough to come down to dinner, but she's better. Go up and see her later. She'd like to say good-bye to you. Her room is forty-six."

When he left them to go to his own table Alice shook her head backwards and forwards muttering, "It doesn't make sense. Nothing makes sense."

"But why are they going, Daddy?" Margaretta demanded.

"I haven't the faintest idea, my dear. The Thorpes have always been a little odd, as you know. One thing, they seem to have no finanical worries. Where are you going, my sweet?"

Alice had flung her napkin down and stood up.

"Excuse me, Dundas, please. I've had a wonderful dinner. I couldn't eat or drink another thing. But I must go up and see Katherine this minute. Because I just can't understand this." She pressed her hands to her temples. "I sometimes think it must be I who is a little odd."

Katherine called, "Come in," in her light sweet voice when Alice tapped at her door. After a moment's hesitation Alice opened the door and walked into the room.

Katherine was sitting up in bed reading. She looked pale and tired, her beautiful eyes without luster and her hands on the book as thin as seabeaten shells. She said in a pleased voice, "Hello, Alice. What are you doing here? I didn't know you were staying in town. If one can call this town. Isn't it an odd little place? It depresses me, all those tumbledown buildings that once were full of life. I like *gay* places, not ones that died fifty years ago. Thank goodness at last Dalton has consented to move."

Something about her quick high voice puzzled Alice. She was talking too much. She accepted Alice's presence too easily, as if she were accustomed to people she knew materializing out of thin air wherever she went.

"Your brother said you had been ill," Alice said. "Are you better now?"

"Yes, quite better, thank you. But I'm so glad to be going away. It was ridiculous of Dalton to try to be a farmer. He knew nothing about it. But it took him until two days ago to realize that. So we decided to move."

"So quickly?"

"Oh, we always go quickly when we've made up our minds. We're going to Australia this time."

Australia. That was where Camilla was. That was

where Felix would be. It was absurd of her to think that there would be any connection between the three.

At random she said, "You're taking Mrs. Jobbett with you?"

Katherine frowned slightly. "Yes, Mrs. Jobbett always comes everywhere with us. Dalton insists. When I protest he says, 'Where would you be without her?' And I suppose that's true."

"Tottie was pleased with her gift," Alice improvised.

Katherine looked up, her wide eyes curious.

"Oh? Did Dalton give Tottie something? But he's always giving people things. I can't stop him."

"Camilla, too?" Alice suggested deliberately.

Katherine's face darkened. Her mouth drooped. She looked as if she were going to cry.

"Camilla was different. She meant a great deal to us. She was the first friend I had had for years. But you see how she treated us? That's really what made me ill again." Her eyes beseeched Alice. "Dalton says I mustn't talk of her any more. So I'm going to forget her. You know, I thought we might be friends. You have a soft voice and you're gentle. I like gentle people. But here I am being whisked away before I have a chance to know you. It's always like that. I'm sorry we didn't even have a chance to have you visit."

"But you—" Alice was beginning. Something in Katherine's face, a queer blank look, stopped her. She listened to Katherine saying, "So good-bye, Alice. It was nice of you to come and see me."

She held out her hand, and Alice felt its brittle dry

thinness in her own. It was limp and yet sharp, like a naked bird. The book Katherine had been reading slid off the eiderdown. Alice stooped to pick it up. Her eye caught the title. It was a girl's school story by Angela Brazil.

Alice went slowly back to her room. She sat on the edge of the bed and tried to think. Her head was muzzy from the wine. She could reconstruct the day's events, but she couldn't put them together intelligently. Her mind was a blur of voices and faces: Mr. Smale's pop-eyed bewilderment about his daughter; the old clergymen with his saint-like face and his gentle rapt interest in Camilla's romantic tendencies; Dundas' queer sharp anger because she had done something he knew nothing about; Dalton Thorpe's narrow medieval face bearing no cruelty, only a tired distant friendliness; and lastly Katherine's high empty voice talking too quickly, her bony hands clutching at the schoolgirls' book. Alice leaned back on her pillows and closed her eyes and the faces went around and around in a slow circle, their mouths opening and shutting, their voices ringing in her ears.

She had had a little too much to drink. It was a nuisance, because she felt that some vital knowledge was within her grasp if only she could concentrate properly. The Thorpes were going to Australia, leaving the tall white house in which she had thought Camilla was hidden empty. Felix was going to Australia; Camilla was there already. At least, Camilla must be there because Dundas had her forwarding address.

Alice sat up sharply. She was suddenly remembering the two letters Miss Wicks had given her for Camilla. They were still in her bag. She had forgotten all about them.

She reached for her bag and took the letters out. One bore a Hokitika postmark, the other an Auckland one. Yesterday she had fully intended to give them to Dundas to forward, but now, all at once, she realized how foolish that would have been. Here, within her hands, lay what might be information that would lead to the solving of the mystery surrounding Camilla's disappearance. It was obviously her duty to open the letters.

Without bothering to argue with her conscience Alice ripped the envelope open.

The Auckland letter was from a firm of solicitors. It read:

DEAR MISS MASON,
   re the Estate of the late Maud Mason
   We do not seem to have received your receipt for the sum of £1189 10s. 6d. forwarded to you by check on the 16th December last, and representing your share in the estate of your late cousin. We would be obliged if you would sign and return to us immediately the enclosed form of receipt.
   Yours faithfully,
      BAILEY, HENDERSON & Co.

Alice's first thought was one of pleasure that old Cousin Maud had turned up trumps for Camilla at last and left her a little money. It was little more than a thousand pounds, and not a great deal as money went nowadays, but to Camilla, who had always scraped along from week to week on her salary, it would be a small fortune. She must have been greatly excited about it and had no doubt been waiting to tell Alice the good news when Alice arrived. It must have been a tremendous effort to keep it a secret, as Camilla had always burst out with everything. It was almost certain that she would have discussed her good fortune with other people.

Other people. The three D's. A little thin eerie voice sounded in Alice's memory. *Lend it to me....*

Webster! The magpie, with his uncanny fluency, repeating a sentence that he must have heard spoken persuasively a great many times. ...Webster who had had his neck wrung. ...

The apprehension was coming back, clinging over Alice like a cobweb.

Dalton Thorpe must find a sister with fastidious tastes, and servants whom it became necessary to bribe, very expensive. Felix was penniless, and was longing to get his company together again. Dundas was a hoarder. ...

Camilla had written, *Things are getting a bit dangerous.* But why, Alice wondered, was she imagining that that comparatively small amount of money represented danger? Camilla's danger more likely lay in her incorrigible flirtation with three men at the same time. It surely couldn't have come from poor Cousin Maud's innocent legacy.

Her head was buzzing as she tore open the other letter.

All it contained, however, was a bill:

"*Dec.* 30 1 *flame-colored nylon nightdress* £4.4.0."

Alice thought of lying in bed in the flame-colored nightdress listening to Dundas' nervous ardent proposal of marriage. That was when her apprehension really became a fear.

She sat with the slip of paper crumpled in her hands listening to someone tapping at the door.

XVII

At last her voice came out with a high-pitched unfamiliar sound.

"Come in," she said.

She thought that if it were Dundas she might scream. But it was only Margaretta.

Margaretta was still overcome with the wine and inclined to giggle.

"Have you gone to bed?" she asked. "Daddy's awfully disappointed. He's nuts about you, really. You should have heard him when he thought you might have disappeared. I thought he would go mad."

"What made him think I might have disappeared?" Alice asked curiously.

"Oh, I suppose Camilla's precedent. It's shaken him a bit. Where did you go, anyway?"

There was no reason, thought Alice, why Margaretta shouldn't know where she had been or what she had heard. She felt quite sober now, and she was interested in the effect of her story on the girl. Slowly and deliberately she related all she had heard that afternoon.

It was curious to watch the change in Margaretta's face. A few minutes ago she had been flushed and giggling; now her mouth fell open, her blurred eyes began to express bewilderment, and, presently, a fear that she tried to conceal. She dropped her eyelids and stared at her hands as Alice repeated again the odd fact that Camilla had been making arrangements for an elaborate wedding in Hokitika.

Finally she burst out with, "You don't believe Camilla is in Australia, do you? Then if she's not there, where is she?"

Alice met her distressed defiant eyes.

"Margaretta, where did you get that nylon night-dress you lent me?"

The swift dark color flew into Margaretta's face.

"I had it. I'd never worn it."

"But where did you get it? Come now, you must tell me, because look, I have a bill here for a nylon nightdress that Camilla bought. It's the same one, of course. Isn't it?"

Margaretta gaped, her eyes losing their defiance. Then she cried, "It's no business of yours! It's no business of yours! You want to know too much. But if you must know I stole it."

"Stole it!"

"Yes. It was so pretty and I'd never had pretty things. You know I hadn't. I took it one day when Camilla was in school. I expected she'd find out some time, but she didn't because she went away just after that."

"Then did you steal those shoes, too, or did

Camilla really leave them because it was a wet night?"

"I don't know anything about the shoes. I hadn't seen them before." Suddenly Margaretta thrust her clenched fists into her eyes and sobbed, "I wish I'd never lent that nightdress to you. You supect everything." Then she turned and rushed out of the room.

Everything, thought Alice wearily, ended in this blank wall. Had Margaretta really stolen the nightdress? She hardly thought the girl had enough ingenuity to make up a story like that, yet neither did she think Margaretta was the type of girl to steal anything. She had a stubborn defiant honesty beneath her subterfuge. Then what was it all about?

Suddenly she remembered the line in Camilla's diary. *They say Margaretta adores her father. . . .* Was that the key?

If things had been getting dangerous for Camilla, Alice felt that now, because of her inquisitiveness, they must be doubly dangerous for her. But it never occurred to her to walk out of the hotel and out of the tangled tortuous lives of this group of people. She would see this thing through even if it meant that Dundas would have another unused wedding dress to store in his attic. Poor Dundas, who was really deeply in love with her.

All night Alice had troubled dreams. The last one was of Felix waving good-bye to her, his mouth laughing, but his eyes having the brilliance of frosty stars. She woke with that awful sense of desolation that came to her at unguarded moments. How could Felix have walked out and left her like this? He must have known that she wasn't in love with Dundas;

that other circumstances, her weakness and loneliness, and, above all, the queer pervading influence of Camilla, had led her into this position. Quite apart from what was happening to her, he might have stayed until the mystery surrounding Camilla was completely cleared up. Unless he had a guilty conscience. . . .

Alice impatiently shook herself awake. She got out of bed and rinsed her face in cold water and brushed her hair. It was depressing how a sad dream clung to one. But it was the effect of the wine she had drunk. She had had no more than a restless night. Poor Margaretta was likely to have a bad hangover.

Remembering Margaretta, Alice decided to go and see how she was. She put on her housecoat and went to tap on Margaretta's door.

There was no answer to her first tap. Alice knocked louder and waited. A maid came along the corridor. She looked at Alice and said, "The young lady in twenty-three has left, miss."

"Left!" Alice repeated. "When?"

"About an hour ago. She was catching the early bus to Greymouth."

Without answering, Alice opened the door and went into the room. Sure enough it was empty both of Margaretta and her luggage. Alice looked around in bewilderment. Then she saw the letter propped on the dressing-table. She snatched it up and read her name on the envelope.

Thank goodness, at least the girl had had the sense to leave a note and had not just vanished into the blue like Camilla had. Alice tore the envelope open and read:

DEAR ALICE,

I am writing to you because I know you will explain to Daddy for me. Suddenly I have been so afraid that he might not keep his promise to let me go to the medical school that I am leaving now and I will get a job until university opens. If I go back with you today Daddy might change his mind, or you might change yours about marrying him, and I will be stuck again. I must go. Please understand.

MARGARETTA.

P.S. I like you very much, and I am sorry I have been rude to you. (I have enough money left from the fifty pounds Daddy gave me.)

They had all told her to go away, Alice thought dazedly, but instead they were going and she was the one to be left. Camilla, Felix, the Thorpes, Margaretta. . . .

With a lurch of her heart, Alice realized that only she and Dundas would be left.

But she had forgotten Miss Wicks. Miss Wicks was most certainly there, for a few minutes after her discovery of Margaretta's flight a message came up for her that she was wanted on the telephone. She hurried down and picked up the receiver to hear Miss Wicks' rapid excited voice: "Is that you, Alice, dear? Are you coming back today?"

"I don't know," said Alice, thinking of Margaretta. "I think so." She lowered her voice. "But I am no further forward, although things have happened."

"Things have certainly happened, my dear. I have a telegram. Camilla is coming back today. I must see Mr. Hill. I shall want to know my position. Is he there now?"

"But—are you sure—I mean, the telegram—is it genuine?"

"I don't see how it couldn't be. It's addressed to the school and it says, 'Arriving about midday Wednesday. Will explain everything. Camilla Mason.' "

"But she's married," Alice said foolishly. "Her name won't be Mason now. It must be a hoax."

"Well, someone is arriving," said Miss Wicks practically. "And since I don't know your friend Camilla I think you ought—"

A hand was laid on Alice's shoulder.

"Good morning, my sweet," came Dundas' affectionate voice, temporarily blotting out Miss Wicks' excited prattle.

Alice swung around.

"Dundas, Camilla is coming back today! I can't believe it! But isn't it wonderful! I'm sorry, Miss Wicks—wait a minute, will you? Dundas is here. I'll get him to speak to you."

She was so full of excitement and pleasure and relief that Camilla was safe, after all, that for a moment she wasn't aware of Dundas' intense astonishment. He was rapping out questions.

"Where is the telegram from? What time was it sent? Yes, I'll be back today. Yes, definitely. Thank you, Miss Wicks. Good-bye."

As he put down the receiver Alice gripped his arm excitedly.

"It isn't a hoax, is it, Dundas? It can't be. I mean,

who would want to send a telegram?" She saw the deep grooves running diagonally from Dundas' mouth to his chin, and faltered. "You do think it is a hoax?"

"Of course it's a hoax," he snapped. "Camilla's on the other side of the world by now. That woman's a nitwit."

"But who would play a poor joke like that on us?" Alice insisted. "No, I think Camilla is coming. I think it's true. Oh, by the way, I'm so excited about this I'm forgetting about Margaretta. She's gone."

"Gone?"

Alice took his arm.

"Oh, I'm sorry. I shouldn't have told you so bluntly. She's only decided to go off to university a little earlier. She's frightened something will happen to stop her if she doesn't go now. I don't know why she's so nervous. I suppose it's because she's so crazy to go. Don't be angry with her, Dundas."

Perhaps, she was thinking wildly, perhaps now that Camilla was safe she could go to Australia with Felix after all. It wouldn't matter that he no longer loved her. They had always worked well together and there would be that. They might have a successful tour.

She became aware that Dundas' face was rigid with anger.

"What made her go off like that? What do you know about it?"

The enemy was looking out of his eyes again, the fierce dark person who gave Alice a cold sensation of fear. Instinctively she moved back a pace.

"I don't know anything, Dundas. Except that

business about the nightdress.''

''What about the nightdress?''

How could Margaretta have adored her father if he showed this stern side to her? But who would suspect that in such a gentle good-natured person there was that side?

''The nylon one she lent me. It was really Camilla's. I knew because an account came for it yesterday. So I asked Margaretta where she got it and she said she had stolen it. Such nonsense! I'm quite sure Margaretta wouldn't be a thief under any circumstances. But that's all that happened. Honestly.''

Again she touched his arm pleadingly. ''It doesn't matter that she's decided to go now. She would have to go in two or three weeks, anyway. The whole trouble, darling, is that you gave us too much to drink last night. Neither I nor Margaretta has the head for it. Margaretta will write in a day or two. Let's get some breakfast and we'll talk about Camilla coming back. Isn't she the most exasperating person? I'm awfully afraid she has never been married at all. She would choose the most complicated way of taking an illicit honeymoon. I suppose she did it on that money from poor old Cousin Maud.''

Dundas turned his head very slowly.

''What money?'' he said.

''Oh, of course you wouldn't know. Apparently she got a legacy from her cousin Maud. There was a letter from the solicitors about it. It wasn't much more than a thousand pounds, certainly not enough for anyone to do anything awful to her. Do come and get breakfast, darling. I badly need some coffee.''

She was so lighthearted about Camilla that she had to prattle. She could see that she was irritating Dundas, she whom he had always looked at with such adoration, but she couldn't help it. The news was wonderful. She had to talk about it. Only now did she realize what a weight Camilla's disappearance had been on her. Like one of the lowering black clouds that so often hid those beautiful snowpeaks. And Dundas wasn't saying a word. Neither was he eating much. He drank two cups of strong black coffee and scowled down at his plate.

Of course, he was upset about Margaretta's behavior. That was only natural. What an odd person he was, making his daughter almost a prisoner in her home. He was too possessive, that was the trouble. He was a hoarder with human beings as much as with inanimate objects. It was almost a disease with him. But what a mistake she had made in thinking that he had been in love with Camilla. If he had been he would have been more pleased at the news that she was safe and coming back.

At first Alice had to admit that she had thought the telegram might have been a hoax. But how could it be? Who would send it and for what purpose?

One girl came back and another disappeared. It was all rather humorous, really. At least, Camilla's return freed her from her sense of obligation about Dundas. She knew now that she had been crazy even to toy with the thought of marrying him. If Felix never came back to her she would have no one. She knew that, yet at this moment she could not feel dejected.

How broad and strong Dundas' hands were on the

table. He was not a tall man, but he had always had that appearance of powerful strength. It almost emanated from him as if it were visible. Strength combined with gentleness could be so devastatingly attractive in a man. But if it were not combined with gentleness. . . .

She must tell the Thorpes about Camilla's return. She really should apologize for her suspicions. Except that they had, she hoped, been secret.

Alice gave a little giggle at the absurdity of her imaginings as far as the Thorpes were concerned, and Dundas looked up.

"I've stopped talking," she said engagingly. "But my thoughts are just as incoherent as my chatter was. What a mind I have! What time shall we leave to go back? Do you know, I had no idea Camilla's disappearance had weighed on me so heavily."

"We'll leave as soon as you're ready," Dundas said. "I'll fix the bill now if you'll pack."

"You won't do anything about Margaretta, will you, Dundas?"

"What should I do?" he said heavily.

Poor darling, he was feeling that he had completely failed as a father. That was what was making him so unapproachable. What would he be like when she told him that she found she could not marry him? Alice shied away from that thought. She stood up and said, "I'll be ready in ten minutes."

But she couldn't leave without seeing Katherine Thorpe and telling her that Camilla was safe. She knocked confidently at the door of number forty-six, and opened it gaily without waiting for a voice to bid her enter.

An arm stretched in front of her, barring the way. She found herself looking into Mrs. Jobbett's hard black eyes.

"What do you want?"

Alice drew back. Then, refusing to be intimidated, she said, "I want to tell Miss Thorpe her friend Camilla is safe. The news will do her good."

Mrs. Jobbett stood firmly for a moment. Then suddenly she seemed to come to a decision. She threw open the door and pointed to the bed.

"There you are, miss. If you think anything will do her good by all means try it."

Alice crossed the room and stood looking down into Katherine Thorpe's beautiful vacant eyes. The girl lay flat in bed, twining her fingers together, and muttering a childish prayer, "Now I lay me down to sleep. . . ."

Even her voice was that of a child: flat, meaningless, babbling.

Mrs. Jobbett stood beside Alice, waiting.

"Well," she said.

"Oh, poor thing!" Alice breathed. "Is she often like this?"

"Often enough."

"But why didn't Mr. Thorpe tell me? I'd never have intruded."

"There's them as has their pride," Mrs. Jobbett said. "The Thorpes are a good family. I might say an exalted family. It's natural they don't want things talked about."

But to constantly move around the world, Alice thought in deep pity, to hand expensive bribes to the few outsiders who were expected to hold their tongues. . . . Now she understood the tired sadness in Dalton Thorpe's eyes. He had grown fanatical about protecting his beautiful sister.

"Now I lay me down to sleep . . ." Katherine babbled.

Camilla had known. She had written, *I gave you my word* . . . But all the same she had received the gift of the squirrel coat. Tottie had known, and had loyally kept her mouth shut and gone away. Now she knew, but it didn't matter any longer because the Thorpes were moving on.

"In her good times she is as sane as you or me," Mrs. Jobbett said. "That's why he won't have her shut up. She's been fine for a long time now. It was that Camilla Mason disappearing so mysteriously that brought this attack on. She used to be fond of that girl. Wrote her letters every day. I must say Miss Mason behaved very decently about it all, until she went off without saying a word." (So that passionate note, *I am longing to see you,* had been Katherine's, Alice was thinking.)

"It's no use your trying to talk to her, miss," Mrs. Jobbett said. "She won't understand a word you say."

"I'm so sorry," Alice said helplessly. She was thinking of how Katherine had wanted to dress up Margaretta that night, as if she were a doll. "So sorry. . . ."

XVIII

TREES ON EITHER SIDE shutting out the sun, a gray narrow road that wound and wound like insertion through a green dress. The fat wood-pigeons fluttering low and chortling in rich content, the magnificent emerald tree ferns with trunks as hairy as gorillas dwindling and thinning into bracken as the road ran through stone-gray streams. A smell of dampness and rotting leaves, a glimpse of a lake like broken glass through the thick undergrowth. The sun sliding behind the inevitable low clouds and the road darkening. Always the hum of the engine and the dizzy swerving around curve after curve.

How could it be that this atmosphere of cool damp-smelling greenness had quite diminished her confidence? She was back to the uncertainty and apprehension of that day when she had stood on the doorstep of the cottage knocking uselessly at the door that never opened. How could she believe that Camilla had come back when she had so completely vanished?

Since leaving Hokitika Dundas had said scarcely a word. He was slightly hunched over the wheel, his thick strong fingers gripping it harder than was necessary. He was driving too fast, and Alice felt her head spinning from the constant curves in the road.

She leaned back and forced herself to think of pleasant things: that time on the ship when, after rehearsing them for hours and bawling them all out, Felix had suddenly looked at her and said with extreme gentleness, "Come on, little Alice," and they had both known, in that lightning moment, that they were in love; the time she had found Felix sitting in the empty theater, a lonely figure in the dress circle, after the play was over and the meager audience had gone home, and he had suddenly caught her to him and kissed her violently and muttered, *"Madame, you have bereft me of all words, only my blood speaks to you in my veins,"* and she had had a dazed radiant feeling that they were still in the play, and that for the rest of their lives they would remain in that felicitous state; the time things were going more and more badly and she was sitting in a small tea-shop with her tears dropping into her coffee, and Felix had said, "You have the most charming baby face when you cry. . . ."

"What are you thinking of?" came Dundas' voice unexpectedly in the rich affectionate velvet tones that almost hypnotized her.

His sudden breaking of the silence between them made her open her eyes sharply.

"Nothing in particular."

"You were smiling."

"Dundas, how can you watch my expression when

you're driving on a road like this?''

The road was climbing tortuously over Mount Hercules. The wooded slopes stretched on either side, forests of beech and rimu and matai, tangled, crowding, ceaselessly green.

''When we're over the hill I know where we can have a picnic lunch. I brought some food. You didn't know I would think about it, did you?''

Indeed, she hadn't known. No one, she thought, had been in less of a mood for a picnic.

''No, I didn't. I thought you were too worried about Margaretta.''

''Oh, Margaretta.'' He gave a sigh. ''One has to be fair. Perhaps I haven't always been.''

Alice was tremendously relieved about his change of mood.

''That's sweet of you, Dundas. I knew you'd begin to see it that way. After all, Margaretta is grown up now and entitled to do as she wants.'' She diplomatically changed the subject. ''A picnic lunch will be lovely. But we're in a hurry. Don't we want to get back to see Camilla?''

''Camilla can wait an hour or two. We can't allow her to intrude on our time. What were you thinking of when you were smiling?''

''Oh, nothing much. I'm a notorious day-dreamer.''

''Was it by any chance that bus driver? An impudent likable fellow I thought he was.''

Alice felt the color creep into her cheeks.

''Felix?'' she said innocently.

''There was something between you two once, wasn't there?'' Dundas said pleasantly.

Alice resented his right to question her—besides the fact that that spot was too sore for probing.

"Perhaps there was, just as there was between you and Miss Jennings. I had never got to the stage of getting a wedding dress," she added.

Instantly she was sorry, not because she had hurt his feelings but because his lips were clamped shut in that frightening manner again.

"What's over is over," she ventured. "Anyway, I wasn't thinking of Felix, but of poor Katherine Thorpe. I hadn't guessed what was wrong with her, and yet now it seems astonishing that I never did. She had that awfully neurotic manner."

"I knew at once," Dundas said. The amiability was still in his voice, as if he were determined to keep it there.

"You knew! And you never told me!"

"My dear girl, can't you realize the dark secret they were making of it? One had to respect that."

"But that night—you knew I was terrified out of my wits—you knew I thought they had done something to Camilla."

"But you couldn't seriously have thought that for long, could you?"

Dundas patted her knee with his heavy square hand and smiled at her amiably.

"In about half an hour we are coming to a tiny, very beautiful lake. I thought we would have lunch there. I wangled a bottle of Sauternes out of the barkeeper. Look, the sun's going to shine, too." Again his hand stole over her knee and he used her own words, "What's over is over, eh?"

Alice nodded a little hypnotically. She was trying

hard to follow his line of reasoning. He loved her, yet he preferred her to spend several days in miserable apprehension and dread rather than betray the secret of people who meant nothing to him.

She wanted to wriggle away from his hand, but couldn't persuade herself to do so. He was such a volcanic person today. The least irritation set him scowling.

(It could be that he had been glad for the incident that caused all her suspicions to rest on the Thorpes. . . . But, no, Camilla was safe, safe!)

"You do love me, don't you, my sweet? Say you do, just to let me hear it in your voice."

Alice was intensely uncomfortable.

"Dundas, I—" She abruptly stopped what she had been going to say and began to chatter. "Do you know, when I first got here I thought you were in love with Camilla. I thought everyone was—Dalton Thorpe and Felix, too. And now I find that none of you were. Poor Camilla was a complete dupe, wasn't she? But you must have led her to believe you cared about her from the things she wrote in her diary. The poor girl! It wasn't fair. And she had that money, too. If it was found that she had been bumped off for her money I am afraid it would be you they would suspect, Dundas."

"Why me?" came his deep lazy voice.

"Because you are the hoarder. Felix hasn't a bean and cares less, and the Thorpes seem to have pots of money. So there you are. Elementary, eh?"

It had been a roundabout way to take him off the subject of whether or not she loved him, but it seemed to have succeeded. For he was smiling in his old pleasant way and saying, "What a fascinating creature you are. What a mind inside that pint-sized body! But if you are going to say horrible things like that about me I think perhaps it would be better if you went right back to sleep."

It was so nice that Dundas was in a pleasant mood again. Alice relaxed and began to think of the possibility of joining Felix in Australia. But what was Dundas going to say? She had to tell him soon. There was no doubt that he would be deeply hurt, but that he would behave in a decent gentlemanly way. She would tell Camilla of the stupid fix she had got into, indirectly because of Camilla herself. Camilla would giggle and give her some airy advice. . . .

"This is where we turn in to the lake," came Dundas' voice. He directed the car into a soft rutty track that ran beneath low-hanging trees for half a mile or so until it came out into an open space on the shores of the miniature lake. There was a tumbledown boathouse and a rowboat pulled up on the shingle bank—that was all.

"No one comes here," said Dundas. "Isn't it an enchanting spot?"

Alice looked at the stretch of water shining darkly from the reflection of the surrounding bush. In the very center like a picture in a frame, there was a small patch of shining blue, and one white lovely mountain peak. It was a mirage in the dark green water, a jewel, the kind of thing one would dive deep to reach.

"If no one comes here, who owns the boat?" Alice said practically.

"It belongs to a neighboring farmer. But he's away

at present. Shall we have lunch first or shall we have a row across the lake?''

"Eat," said Alice contentedly. She threw herself down on the sun-warmed shingle. "If you give me some of that Sauternes I'll think I'm in heaven."

"That's what—" Dundas stopped rather abruptly, as if his tongue had momentarily been going to betray something. "That's where I am now," he finished blandly. "Sunshine, food, a beautiful stretch of water, the loveliest girl I have ever seen. . . ."

"Come off it," said Alice. "I'm not even pretty."

"My dear, to me you are matchless. So little, so perfect. Maybe we had better eat before I grow too lyrical."

He produced the package of sandwiches and the bottle of wine from the car. It was worthy of record, Alice thought humorously, that for the space of fifteen minutes Felix's dark-browed face did not come into her mind once. Some day she would tell him that. She would say, "I was lying on the shore of a marvelous lake with a man who loved me passionately, getting slowly and delightfully drunk."

"What would you do if you found I didn't love you after all, Dundas?" she asked lightly, when it no longer seemed to matter what she said.

He eyed her with eyes grown yellow in the sunlight. *Tiger's eyes,* Alice thought lazily.

"I would row you out and tip you into the bottom of the lake. And it's a very deep lake. Deep and cold." He was giving his mild little laugh. "Come along, let's row, anyway, before we go to sleep."

"Camilla," Alice murmured.

"What about her?"

"We have to get back to see her."

"Oh, she can wait. Waiting won't hurt her."

He pushed the boat into the water, and she climbed in. It was a very small boat and it rocked as they pushed off. Dundas grasped the oars competently. They made a pleasant cool sound in the water. The distance from the shore steadily increased. Alice trailed her hand. It was true, the water was very cold, icy cold, as if that mirrored snowpeak had frozen it.

"In the middle," Dundas said, "the depth hasn't been measured."

"That was where that lovely picture of the sky and the mountains was. I wonder if we can see it when we are over it."

"Lean over and see," Dundas suggested, "See, I'll stop rowing. The ripples spoil the reflections. Let's sit here absolutely still."

The ripples on the water widened and widened and vanished. Alice leaned over. The boat rocked softly. The dark-green water moved.

Suddenly the rocking of the boat increased violently. Dundas half fell against her. She was plunged to the armpits in the icy water. Then he was dragging her back, panting, trying to steady the boat.

She fell back into her seat, wet and shivering. Dundas' face was splashed with water, too. Or was it perspiration? His eyes were quite black.

"God! You nearly fell in. You nearly upset the boat when you leaned over so far." He held out his arms as if he wanted to take her into them. His face was distraught.

"But I didn't," Alice said practically. It had been

so quick, too quick to be really frightened. "So don't get so upset. Anyway, I can swim."

"Not in that water," he said. "You'd be frozen before you got to the bank."

"But you're here with the boat, silly. You'd rescue me. All the same, I'm glad I didn't. It looks so dark down there. Let's go back to the shore, shall we?"

After a minute Dundas grasped the oars. His face was still white and twisted.

"So near," he muttered. "And you're the kind of woman I've looked for all my life." He gave a curiously wry smile. "Damn you!" he said. He almost looked as if he were crying.

XIX

MISS WICKS did not seem to be at home. Neither did Camilla. Alice rapped at the front door, and felt the rain from rapidly gathering clouds begin to speckle her face. She could hear faintly the ginger cat mewing inside. She tried the door and found it locked.

With the last sunlight obscured by the clouds it was almost dark. Already moisture was beginning to drop off the shiny leaves of the ngaio tree. Although there was no wind, a cabbage tree was rustling. It sounded like taffeta skirts. It was only the cabbage tree, not Camilla running down the hall to open the door.

The little cottage was empty except for the cat. She was back to where she had been a fortnight ago, with all the oppressive gloom and mystery of the place surrounding her.

There was a step behind her and Dundas stood at her shoulder.

"No one home?" he said.

"There can't be. There are no lights. And I can hear the cat crying."

In the gloom she realized that he was smiling. It was a peculiar smile, not happy, but knowledgeable, ironic, almost sadistic. No, surely that was a trick of the light. She edged away from him.

"Dundas—"

"Did you really expect Camilla to be here?" he asked. "Come. We'll go home."

"But—the telegram—"

"Someone has been playing a trick on us. Couldn't you see that from the start?"

She watched his odd frightening smile.

"Dundas—you sent it!"

He shook his head.

"No. But I intend to find out who did. I think probably it was Margaretta. She would think it a very funny joke. You wouldn't have suspected she would have a sense of humor like that, would you? Never mind, we won't hold it against her."

He took her arm. His strong fingers closed around it tightly. His voice was deeper than it had ever been, the thickest, softest, most suffocating black velvet. He was still smiling.

"It must have been Margaretta," he said. "She was the only one who might have known."

Alice tried to draw away from him. Her heart was beating violently.

"Known what?" she whispered.

"What are you frightened of, love?" came his velvet voice. "Don't you know that I adore you? Come on home. Margaretta," he added, with a slight chuckle, "knew nothing at all."

Now at last all her vague apprehensions and suspicions had crystallized into the deadliest fear. Her mind flung her chaotic sentences. *I wonder if it's true what they say about Dundas. Margaretta adores her father. It's getting a bit dangerous.* 1 *flame-colored nylon nightdress* £4.40.

She had sense enough to know that at this minute it was useless to resist him. She could only pin her slender hopes on the mysterious sender of that telegram (if it were not Margaretta), and the fact that Dundas, in his unbalanced way, really did worship her. What a blind fool she had been, she who thought she was being so clever and constructive. What a silly little lamb, Felix would have said.

"Felix!" she whispered desperately, as if his name on her lips might be a charm.

They were in the car and Dundas was driving rapidly around the bend in the road up to his own gate. He swept into the drive, the headlights flashing on the scarlet and yellow dahlias. There was a riot of color, then the dark tree-trunks, then the lighted windows of the house.

Lighted! Who had turned on the lights?

Dundas stopped the car and sat quite still. The blinds of the windows were drawn, but chinks of light showed, and the dark-red glass in the hall door blazed crimson.

"It can't be Margaretta," Alice murmured aloud. "She's gone."

Excitement and relief were mounting in her. She was emerging from that brief nightmare.

"Dundas, it really is Camilla."

"It can't be Camilla!" he snapped, and leapt out of the car.

Alice followed him as quickly as she could in view

of the way her legs were trembling. She reached the front door just as Dundas had opened it and was stepping inside.

Someone was singing in a deep exaggerated croon: *"Night and da-aay, you are the o-oone. . . ."*

Camilla's theme song! They had always teased her about it. She had said it was her best parlor trick. There was no doubt at all that she still used it.

"Camilla!" Alice cried joyfully, pushing past Dundas and bursting into the hall.

The staircase ran up into the gloom of the un-lighted first floor. Someone was coming down it—a woman. She paused just on the edge of the shadow. Then she gave a mischievous giggle, and, turning, ran back up the stairs.

It *was* Camilla. Alice had seen the gray squirrel coat and the long blonde hair. But how peculiarly she was behaving.

"Camilla, you idiot!" she called, and began running towards the stairs.

"Stop here!" said Dundas curtly. He had seized her arm and was holding her in a hard grip.

Alice struggled furiously. "Let me go! Camilla's upstairs. She's—" Her voice died away as she saw Dundas' face, pallid and glistening. Why, he was terrified! But what had he done that he should be terrified of Camilla?

Before she knew what was happening she found herself being pushed with all the strength in Dundas' short powerful body into the living-room. She stumbled on a rug and half fell. As she recovered herself she saw an extraordinary sight.

There were two women in the room sitting quietly by the empty hearth. They looked as if they were chatting. One had her hand half outstretched to the other. The extraordinary thing was that they were both dressed in bridal gowns with veils spreading filmily over their shoulders.

Alice pressed her fingers to her eyes and took them away again. Now she was imagining things. It *had* been Camilla on the stairs, but these two frozen figures were not real. They were simply life-sized versions of the Dresden china figures that stood like snowflakes about the room.

She was aware of a peculiar sound behind her. It was Dundas giving an exclamation that was half cry, half a sharp intake of breath. He stood quite still, and suddenly his face had a sunken look. He looked very old, very very tired. His mouth sagged at the corners. He was almost about to weep, an old man with a small boy's piteous expression.

Then, very quietly, so that Alice was scarcely aware of what he was doing, he stepped backwards into the hall, closing the door as he went. There was a small click as the key turned in the lock.

It took her a moment to realize that she was locked in with those two strange brides, their chatter arrested in mid-sentence, their very attitude in keeping with this horrible museum-like room. She took a tentative step towards them, and saw, as she had suspected, that the figures were dummies, with the exaggerated eyelashes and coarse black hair of shop-window models.

Who had brought them here and why? It seemed

such an odd joke to play on Dundas. Why should it have startled him so much that he had locked her in and gone?

Too much had happened. Her brain was so weary that she could not think intelligently. She could just stare at the silent white figures so strangely by Dundas' fireside. Two brides. Why, of course. . . . She could recognize the wedding dresses that Margaretta had shown her: her mother's white satin in the style of the early forties and that other slightly discolored lace of the mysterious Miss Jennings, who had disappeared. The girl who hadn't been a bride after all. . . .

Camilla had chattered vivaciously to the Reverend Adam Manners of a white wedding. Had she been a bride? *Had she?*

Alice herself, in one foolish hour, had contemplated becoming the mistress of this house with its queer trophies.

And suddenly, with dreadful clarity, Alice saw the whole thing. These petrified figures belonged to this room just as much as the luster bowls and the crystal and silver did. For they had contributed the contents of the room. Certainly Margaretta's mother who had slipped down a crevasse on the glacier had, and now Alice was almost sure that Miss Jennings, who had never even contrived to get a wedding ring on her finger, had added her share. And Camilla's thousand pounds from Cousin Maud was going to add more museum pieces, perhaps a Persian rug or a pair of Queen Anne candlesticks. Dundas would have his grim souvenirs, for hoarding was a disease with him. He couldn't bear to destroy anything, not even an incriminating nylon nightdress or a pair of black suède shoes. Camilla must have had a suitcase packed that day she had gone to Hokitika with Dundas to cash her check and, as she thought, to marry Dundas, and he had been lured into keeping its contents. He took the most absurd and unnecessary risks.

Where did she herself come in? Of course, she was an heiress. She, unlike Miss Jennings and Camilla, would get as far as the gold band on her finger because the thing would have to be legitimate. When Dundas had thought she had six brothers he had urged her to go away, but when he had discovered that she was the only child of wealthy parents who lived a safe distance away the situation had been entirely different. She remembered his enveloping warmth the night he had asked her to marry him, the kindness that she had thought was so selfless and sincere, and abruptly she began to tremble.

At any moment he might come back into this haunted room. And now he would have no mercy. He would have to dispense with her fortune because it was too dangerous to wait for it. Knowing what she did, how could she expect to be allowed to live?

All at once, over her head, someone began to laugh. Camilla's provocative laugh. Was it? Alice couldn't be sure. Before she had identified the sound Dundas' voice sounded in a violent protest.

"Be quiet! Please! Please be quiet!" It died into an agonized whisper. "*Please?*" Then abruptly the front door banged. There was the sound of a car starting, and after that footsteps upstairs. Suddenly someone was running down the stairs. Coming nearer and nearer. . . .

Alice jerked into life, made a dash for the windows. Thank heaven this was a downstairs room. Thank heaven! She could climb out of the window and run. Hide in the bush. Try to get as far as the hotel.

The window was locked. Kneeling on the couch underneath it she struggled desperately with the old-fashioned lock. It yielded at last. She was just pushing up the frame when the door behind her opened.

It was no use. In imagination she was already out of the window and flying for hiding—but her limbs refused to move. She stood like a caught burglar.

"Little Alice!" came Felix's caressing voice. "Silly little lamb! You see, it took the sheep in wolf's clothing to rescue you."

Alice half turned. Felix's thin tender face, his ruffled black hair, swam before her vision. But Felix was in Australia! No, he wasn't. He wouldn't leave her. Of course he wouldn't leave her. . . .

"Felix!" she cried. "You know it's no use without you. No use at all. . . ." Her voice died away and she sank gracefully onto the period couch with its tapestry of enormous faded pink roses.

XX

STRANGELY ENOUGH it was Miss Wicks' voice she could hear.

"Poor little kid! What a shame to give her such a fright!"

"She'll be all right. She's tough, is little Alice."

That was Felix's cheerful voice, and with it Alice's eyes opened wide.

She had never completely lost consciousness, but that quiet dim interval in which her senses wavered had somehow erected a barrier between the horror of the still room and the doomed brides and the intense comfort of Felix's presence.

Miss Wicks seemed to have some extraordinary yellow mass hanging crookedly on top of her head. Beneath it her sharp eyes twinkled kindly; the tip of her nose trembled with a life all its own. She seemed to have a fur coat on, too. . . .

Alice shot up.

"It was you!" she said, pointing accusingly at the gray squirrel coat, at the lopsided blonde wig. Then her voice broke in grief. "It wasn't Camilla after all."

Felix sat beside her and put his thin warm nervous hand over hers.

"I'm afraid it never will be Camilla," he said briskly. Characteristically, he refused to let her brood. "I'm sorry about those horrible women"—he indicated the dummies—"but luckily we didn't have to include you in the Madame Tussaud exhibition. And well we may have had to, the way you've been acting, little stupid."

Alice looked around sharply.

"Where's Dundas?"

"I should think on the glacier by this time. Didn't you hear his car? He went off hell for leather."

Alice's mouth was dry. She felt sick.

"But—why the glacier? Is he—"

Felix said calmly, "I've telephoned the hotel and they're sending a couple of guides. But I think they may be too late." He paused. "Let's hope they are."

Alice could see the tiny black figures struggling over the ice, disappearing behind knife-sharp pinnacles, coming out again into the dusk, flies on a wall, climbing higher and higher to the deepest crevasses. . .

"Camilla?" she whispered.

"She never went to Australia," said Felix. "She never left here except to go into Hokitika one day in Dundas Hill's car to cash a check. They remembered her at the bank because she insisted on having over a thousand pounds in cash. After that, no one seems to have seen her again."

"She didn't get the mothballs," Alice said

stupidly. "They were for the fur coat, like I said."
She blinked tiredly. "Dundas hadn't sent the coat
away, after all."

"He hadn't sent anything away. After all, he had
nowhere to send it, had he? It was just awfully bad
luck for him that you arrived at the cottage right on
top of Camilla's disappearance. He hadn't had time
to do a thing. He had wanted undisturbed days to
ponder over what he would destroy, what a prudent
chap like him would keep. But you arrived and
ruined all his pleasant anticipation. He tried to turn
you out of the cottage. But you stuck. Like a limpet.
It was a horrible nuisance at first, but then he found
out you had a wealthy family a long way away, and
he thought, 'What luck! Here old Dundas falls on his
feet again!' It was luck, because in the meantime you
had very nearly been killed with the branch of a tree
falling on you in a storm."

Alice remembered the door of the cottage opening
behind her into blackness.

"You mean—it wasn't accidental?"

Felix's eyes had their frosty brilliance.

"*Murder most foul,*" he said.

"And yet you went away and left me?"

"My dear, the moment I heard you were engaged
to the devious Mr. Hill I knew you were absolutely
safe, safe indeed until your parents died. Especially
since I think he really had an infatuation for you.
Besides, as you see, I didn't go away. But you con-
veniently took Mr. Hill to Hokitika, leaving the coast
clear for Miss Wicks and me to have a private inves-
tigation of our own."

Alice tried to smile.

"Yes, he was crazy about me. If he hadn't been—" She stopped. Suddenly, in another moment of illumination, she saw his hastily repented attempt to tip her into the lake, his crazed snatching at her because never before had he killed a woman he really loved.

"Felix, you haven't found Camilla?"

"N-no," he answered, reluctant now for her to realize the ultimate horror.

"Then I know where she is." She spoke almost dreamily. "Right in the center of the lake there's a little patch of water that catches the sun. It's like a shining blue mirror. I'm glad that was the spot where Camilla would go—down into blueness. . . ."

She heard Dundas' agonized voice pleading, "Be quiet! Please be quiet!" and knew exactly how it had happened, how he couldn't bear Camilla's screams and had had to press his fingers deeper and deeper. . . .

Felix caught her to him.

"Oh, my darling! My poor little Alice! My wonderful crazy brave little fool!"

That was how one could forget it all, in the tightness of Felix's embrace. Alice buried her face against his tweed jacket, willing herself to stay forever in the intense charm of this moment.

"We're getting out of here," came his voice. "I only got Camilla to ask you to visit because I wanted to keep an eye on you. As you know. I think I must be convinced now that you like having no money. I had to give you time to find that out. Hadn't I? But to hell with it, you're going to marry a poor man in spite of all."

"Try to stop me!" said Alice, her eyes radiant. Then her treacherous memory was catching at her again. "Felix, we must keep an eye on Margaretta. Poor kid, she's suspected this for a long time. I realize that now. That's why she was so rude to me, so I would go away. Camilla said she had adored her father. She was trying to convince herself that none of the things she had found meant anything. But she played fair. When she knew I was staying she showed me everything: the nylon nightdress that Carmilla must have bought that day in Hokitika, those pathetic wedding dresses. She couldn't show me what Dundas was burning that night when I was ill. It must have been something that got—marked."

"Stop thinking," said Felix, kissing her on the lips.

Alice caught a movement out of the corner of her eye. It was Miss Wicks methodically divesting the models of their white finery.

"Oh, Miss Wicks! I'd—we'd forgotten you were here."

"Don't mind me, dear. I'm deaf and blind. But we have to get these models back to the shop in Hokitika. They're only hired. Mr. Dodsworth arranged for that. He drove all night to get them here in time. But it was my suggestion about the telegram. I had a feeling you might get scared in Hokitika and walk out, and who could have blamed you? We wanted to make sure you came back." Her sharp eyes twinkled. "Didn't we, Mr. Dodsworth?"

"Miss Wicks, don't be obvious. It's unworthy of a subtle creature like you. Do you know, Alice, she has hidden talent? Didn't you hear her rendering of Camilla's song after only one coaching? It was masterly."

Miss Wicks blushed pink with pleasure. The end of her nose quivered madly .

"What I say is, why don't we all come over to my place, for a nice cup of tea?"

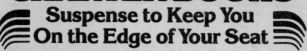

Don't Miss these Ace Romance Bestsellers!

_____#75157 **SAVAGE SURRENDER** $1.95
The million-copy bestseller by Natasha Peters,
author of Dangerous Obsession.

_____#29802 **GOLD MOUNTAIN** $1.95

_____#88965 **WILD VALLEY** $1.95
Two vivid and exciting novels by
Phoenix Island author, Charlotte Paul.

_____#80040 **TENDER TORMENT** $1.95
A sweeping romantic saga in the
Dangerous Obsession tradition.

Available wherever paperbacks are sold or use this coupon.

ace books,
   Book Mailing Service, P.O. Box 690, Rockville Centre, N.Y. 11571

Please send me titles checked above.

I enclose $ . . . . **Add 50¢ handling fee per copy.**

Name . . . .

Address . . . .

City . . . . State . . . . Zip . . . .

—74B

ROMANTIC SUSPENSE

Discover ACE's exciting new line of exotic romantic suspense novels by award-winning author Anne Worboys:

THE LION OF DELOS

RENDEZVOUS WITH FEAR

THE WAY OF THE TAMARISK

THE BARRANCOURT DESTINY

Coming soon:

HIGH HOSTAGE

HEALTH AND BEAUTY—ADVICE FROM THE EXPERTS

D.E. STEVENSON ROMANCES

"Finding a re-issued novel by D. E. Stevenson is like coming upon a Tiffany lamp in Woolworth's. It is not 'nostalgia'; it is the real thing."

—THE NEW YORK TIMES
BOOK REVIEW

ENTER THE WORLD OF D. E. STEVENSON IN THESE DELIGHTFUL ROMANTIC NOVELS:

AMBERWELL
THE BAKER'S DAUGHTER
BEL LAMINGTON
THE BLUE SAPPHIRE
CELIA'S HOUSE
THE ENCHANTED ISLE
FLETCHERS END
GERALD AND ELIZABETH
GREEN MONEY
THE HOUSE ON THE CLIFF
KATE HARDY
LISTENING VALLEY
THE MUSGRAVES
SPRING MAGIC
SUMMERHILLS
THE TALL STRANGER